In a Galaxy Far, Far AwRy
Issue 1: Serial Fiction Sideshow

Liam Gibbs

IN A GALAXY FAR, FAR AWRY issue 1: SERIAL FICTION SIDESHOW
Copyright © 2015 Liam Gibbs
All rights reserved.

Cover art by Claudiu Limbasan.
Cover art colors by Jesse Heagy.
Cover concept and design by Liam Gibbs.
Cover songs by various artists.

This book, or parts thereof, may not be reproduced in any form without permission.
That goes double for you, Al.

As awesome as this book is, it's a work of fiction. I know, I know. We were all hoping, but it just ain't gonna be. Names, characters, businesses, organizations, places, events, and incidents either are the product of the author's freaky imagination or are used fictitiously. Any resemblances to actual persons, living or dead, events, or locales is entirely bonkers and coincidental. In other words, sadly you can't get Schizophrenic's autograph.

ISBN: 1505375401
ISBN 13: 978-1505375404

First printing: July 2015

{ PLOT DEVICE PUBLISHING }

THE STORY SO FAR...

Issue 1: Serial Fiction Sideshow, available at http://tiny.cc/iagffa1, on inagalaxyfarfarawRy.com, and in the hearts of one and all

Issue 2: Home Sweet Home Invasion, available at http://tiny.cc/iagffa2, on inagalaxyfarfarawRy.com, and also in the hearts of one and all

Issue 3: Technophobia, available at http://tiny.cc/iagffa3, on inagalaxyfarfarawRy.com, an—you're starting to see a pattern here, aren't you?

Issue 4: Armageddon Trigger Finger, available at http://tiny.cc/iagffa4, on inagalaxyfarfarawRy.com, and... hey...your heart. And everyone else's.

OTHER STUFF THE AUTHOR SPEWED OUT

Not So Superpowered, available at tiny.cc/nssuperpowered

Three Flash Fictions, available upon request from the author

Random limericks, available in bathroom stalls

DEDICATED TO...

...my grandfather, William Gibbs.
It's largely his fault you're reading this.

ACKNOWLEDGEMENTS

No book is a one-man job. Let's get that on the table first. Sure, one name goes on the front, but it's still not a one-man job. I drove this thing but I had a ton of backseat drivers. Some were louder than others and one guy yelled at me for swerving into oncoming traffic even though I'd totally do it agai—

My point is, more than a few people helped me along the way. There are way too many to name, but chief among them are the following crazy awesome folks. My heartfelt thanks go out to…

…Matt Levesque, Lieutenant IQ 23's biggest fan, for beta-reading everything—sometimes twice—and commenting on it, even if I never got the decoder ring to figure out what he meant. Thanks for our late-night sessions, hashing out minutiae that might not have even made it into the final product.

…Steve Baptista for beta-reading without complaint and for catching my mistakes when I don't. He remembers so many details I have suspicions he's a robot. Thanks for slogging through all my questions, changes, and concerns, Steve-o-tron 5000.

…Mark Nadon for beta-reading, providing military

advice, and telling me what I could fudge for drama and what I shouldn't. Thanks for egging me into every weekend contest that comes our way.

...LeAnh Gibbs for picking up the slack so I can get this thing done. Thanks for the slack picking up. And for being "there" every time.

...Bernie Pallek for being my campaign manager and sorting out the web site in all its magnificent glory at www.inagalaxyfarfarawRy.com. Thanks for being my Canadian street team.

...Jeffrey Ponzio for helping spread the word to make this happen in the U.S. and online. Thanks for acting as my American tour guide/street team/online megaphone.

...Andrew MacLellan for the insurmountable task of being Andrew MacLellan. Thanks for joining in our stupid antics back in the day. Those antics helped me develop the sense of humor I use today. You helped me through a lot of junk over the years. Love you, brother, no matter where you go.

...Sandy Larabie for the last-minute double-check. Your help was indispensable. Let me know when you're ready for the next one. See you on the jogging circuit!

...Dustin Hayes, Marie Robertson, Oliver Gross, and Colin Atterbury for the help and advice in designing, laying out, and marketing this beast. It's been a long road, but you guys helped me pull through the roadblocks.

...God for giving me this storytelling bug.

…my grandfather, William Gibbs, for urging me into this. If I were a wind-up toy, you were the one who cranked the handle on my back and pointed me in the right direction.

…caffeine.

…not the guy who flipped me the bird on the highway last week. Mean old codger.

AND READERS LIKE YOU...

I want to send some shout-outs to people who helped get this thing shoved into your hands. It was a Kickstarter campaign that made this possible, and with that was a long list of supporters that helped bust open the roof on this project. So here we go in random order. Not alphabetical order. It's had its moment in the sun.

Sue and Phil Gibbs (mum 'n' dad)
Marie Chaput Macdonald
Lele Thai
Heather Puncher
Sergio Baldis

Murielle Cassidy
Wendy Ard
Dark Age Comics
Tawmis Logue
Joe Ponzio

Jay and Silent Bob's Secret Stash, 35 Broad St., Red Deer, NJ
Elite Battlegrounds, 299 Route 22 East, Green Brook, NJ
Amazing Heroes, 966 Stuyvesant Ave., Union, NJ
Comic Fortress, 59 West Main St., Somerville, NJ
Kobold's Corner, 430 Hazeldean Rd., Kanata, ON
Wizard's Tower, 3350 Fallowfield Rd., Ottawa, ON
The Hobby Centre/The Cave, 33 Roydon Pl. #6, Ottawa, ON
The Comic Book Shoppe, 1400 Clyde Ave., Ottawa, ON
The Comic Book Shoppe, 228 Bank St., Ottawa, ON
Anime Stop, 1400 Clyde Ave., Ottawa, ON
Monopolatte, 640 Somerset St. West, Ottawa, ON
Silver Snail, 391 Bank St., Ottawa, ON
Carta Magica, 1179 St. Laurent Blvd., Ottawa, ON
Entertainment Ink, Place D'Orléans Dr., Orléans, ON

Usually the prologue is the beginning of the story and, in a way, so it is with this story. I'm not knocking it. It works...if it's done right. Let's deal with this and keep reading.

Dealt with? Good. It got kind of weird there when you pulled out your hair and yelled, "*What has become of humanity?*" I won't say anything if you don't. I'm glad we found the inner fortitude to move past that.

This series took twenty-five years to make it into your hands. Read that again because that wasn't a misprint: twenty-five long years. You're probably thinking to yourself, *Why twenty-five years?* or *What was this slacker doing that whole time?* or *Should I wear my hair down?* Yes. You should. It's a good look for you.

Let me explain. Twenty-five years ago, give or take, I was a wee lad with no real idea of how the world worked except that I wanted to create something. Not buildings—I had enough Lego for that, anyway—but something unique. A book. And not just one standalone book, but a series. Yeah, a series! A series lets me recycle the characters instead of abandoning them in favor of the next book and then the next and then th—The idea is "Waste not, want not," right?

I wrote that series of books in grade school and high school. Two books and one halfway done with a smattering of shorter stories along the way. In the writing world, there's no truer saying than "The first million words are practice." That adage means you write one million words of shlock before your wordsmithery even *starts* getting good. Just like with dollars, the first million is the hardest. And I was the embodiment of that adage. My two-and-a-half books were unwieldy, 700-page monsters that no publisher would touch from a first-time author. Stephen King can write and sell thousand-page tomes, ones long enough and heavy enough to creak when you open them in libraries. I'm not Stephen King. I had no sense of structure, no sense of storytelling, no sense of timing. My sense of smell wasn't that great either. But I kept editing and editing in the hopes that one day—*one* day—someone would take notice, that I'd get it right. After all, even Stephen King had to write his first million words at some point.

The work was toilsome. Not because I hated the stories, but because I hated reworking my shlock over and over again. I wanted to move forward, not repolish the same stuff a hundred times. But my grandfather encouraged me to keep at it. Hard work is the only worthwhile work. Something like that. And when he read my stuff back to teach me how to improve, he had such a British storyteller's voice that I couldn't help but listen. I remember one time he enunciated the word *burped* with such character he was almost burping the word back to me.

But the tedium overwhelmed me. So I took a breather and wrote an "origin" story to my two-and-a-half-books-with-a-smattering-of-short-stories series. You see, my series had originally started in the middle of this battle between good and evil, like how *Star Wars* started with episode four, with the war already raging. So I decided to go back to the beginning, and this origin story began on day one of the war I was writing.

And this origin story was better than the material it preceded. Funnier. Grander. Shorter and easier to work with. So I finished it. And I didn't stop there. I wrote a follow-up, and then another, and suddenly my two-and-a-half-books-with-a-smattering-of-short-stories series was history. It didn't even fit into the new narrative I'd written. The new narrative was better.

This novella you're holding now is the first issue of that new narrative.

That's right: *you're reading the reboot.* This is *Ultimate Spider-Man*, Michael Bay's *Transformers*, Christopher Nolan's *Batman Begins*, but without previous source material. Will my two-and-a-half-books-with-a-smattering-of-short-stories series ever rear its unwieldy, ugly face? Nope. I won't put it out there. There's not enough money in the world. Some of you have read the stories from that series. Matt, Heather, Bernz, a few others. But those stories are hidden on my computer and in my closet, buried for a reason. Like I said, they're horrible. I might retell them one day—I already adapted one short story into issue five and have plans to stick other elements into future issues—but that original narrative is locked away. Be thankful. It's not pretty.

Twenty-five years later, you've got this. Some of the plot is the same. Much is different. I kept my favorite characters, added new ones, trashed the rest. I tightened up the universe, gave the setting a personality (to me, setting always needs a personality), changed some names, changed some factions, and even swapped one character's gender. But this is the sum total of twenty-five years of sci-fi, comic book, and comedy fandom. Twenty-five years of practice. This story starts my next million words.

My grandfather's not with us anymore. He passed on twenty years this past January. But I get the feeling he'd be proud. After all, he was the person who got me started. This is partly his legacy. And for that, he deserves his name in this novella too. And if he read this story back to me, he'd enunciate every word like he enunciated that burp, British accent and all.

And now on with the (side)show.

In a Galaxy Far, Far AwRy
Issue 1: Serial Fiction Sideshow

CHAPTER ONE
AND THE MAN BEHIND THE OPERATION
WAS NO MORE THAN A WELL-PAID IDIOT

July 19, 9108. 12:54 a.m. (Galactic Standard Time).

Destruction. Wholesale, wanton, razing, galaxywide destruction. Master Asinine *loved* destruction. Especially the wholesale kind, because you could get that at a discount. And he was planning so much of it. Destruction, not discount, for the record.

And maybe a bit of pillaging. He needed to set aside time for his hobbies.

"You know I know you all know why I've called you here," Master Asinine said. Wait. Was that right? I know...you know...

Aboard the titan-class, spacefaring vessel *The Mikazin Starship*, in a room hotly lit using a single overhead light panel, Asinine spoke those introductory words and circled the table at which sat the leaders of six other criminal organizations: Grestlix of the Houdin clan, Markiset of the Watercrest clan, Requiston of the Vobinsix clan, Sikth'nkphth of the R'zext'wixv clan, Wiltroh of the Hygring clan, and Convenient Victim of the Warmaunt clan. Asinine led the Mikazin clan, the most powerful crime syndicate in the galaxy. His second-in-command, a Terran named Lieutenant IQ 23 in the media, and his personal bodyguard, a never-speaking Virillian media-named Braindead, followed him where he paced. He had no clue why they followed so closely. Wherever he walked, those two treated him like a mother duck at a road crossing. Go figure.

Asinine cleared his throat. "You see, we've wasted enough time fighting one another and freaking one another out. Wasted enough firepower. Wasted my Frog Factoid-a-Day desk calendar, thanks to a fluke explosion in my starship's engine room. But now is the time to stop all that waste."

Master Asinine halted. Lieutenant IQ 23 bumped into him from behind, shoving him a step farther.

The six other leaders scowled at each other, their most trusted guards standing vigil behind them in case of treachery. And with good reason: hostility baked this crowd. Feuds had raged for years among these organizations. But Asinine sought to end that hostility. To accomplish that, he had gathered them on his turf, in his starship. Now he had control. He rubbed his hands together maniacally. This was so thrilling it seeped out of his pores. Or maybe that was his skin wax.

Other than the spotlighted table and those surrounding it, nothing was visible. As pronounced as a blood moon, the light panel emitted a beam shrouding everything outside its sharp boundary, as if nothing existed in the blackness beyond. Master Asinine stepped toward the table, showing off his getup: a Mylar bodysuit decorated with yellow and navy-blue splotches that winked in the spotlight when he resumed circling the table. A great and threatening color combination. What he loved most about it was the helmet that hid all but his Terran mouth and chin. Its best feature was a spike at its top. Anything landing on him would ignite in pain. He also used it for shish kebabs.

Wrath in the room oozed from those present like bacon grease from a frying pan. Also, Master Asinine had cranked the heat to give these suckers a reason to sweat. The air felt thick enough to be dissected in a high school lab. One of those household lasers that sliced through tin cans and shoes would work best, but an everyday kitchen laser could also do the trick. Or his nuclear nail clipper.

The leaders evil-eyed Asinine, who paced on heels that thumped in the otherwise soundless room. The time and interest of the criminal leaders sitting here were things few ever obtained. These leaders represented the nastiest crime families in the planetary system of Renovodomus, perhaps even in the whole galaxy of Stratus Cloud. Master Asinine had chosen only the greatest to attend this meeting because he kept all his coolest stuff on this starship. His collection of coolness was meant for the eyes of only a select few.

Or maybe a surgical laser would do it. Those things worked freaky magic.

Asinine read the stone-frozen expressions on the other leaders as though reading nostalgia-store newspaper print with ink that smeared all over your fingers. He reveled in their uneasiness. And these pathetic weasels would soon cower in fear, for none of them had anything as super awesome as a new mind-swap ray. Whatever it did. One hid in his back pocket, and he quivered to refrain from pressing its shiny button marked "Identity Crises for Everybody."

"The crime syndicates represented here attempt to beat the military forces of Renovodomus, but each attempts it alone. Everyone, to be so eloquent, I have the newest, best, most wicked-slickiest domination plan of all time. Here, today, aboard *The Mikazin Starship*, I will create history. And not the kind of history told in classrooms but the kind of history that does cool stuff to other stuff."

Around the table, the leaders eyed each other and snarled silently. Grestlix, the only other Terran leader, squared her jaw at Asinine, who began strolling again with Lieutenant IQ 23 and Braindead following. Braindead's breathing hissed underneath the headgear that revealed his scaly green skin through only an eye slit. He watched everything with the vigilance of a bug-eyed painting.

Asinine drummed his fingers on the table on his next pass. "I'm here to propose something I think you'll all find of interest. I've thought this through, spent many sleepless nights planning, pondering, banging my head against an electrified wall, recovering, wondering if this is really the right thing. And, after several discussions with my lieutenant about having better judgment, I'm going ahead with it, anyway."

He spun around to face them so dramatically that Requiston swiped for his pistol but kept it in its holster. Convenient Victim recoiled with his wiry tail slapped protectively across his chest. If it weren't for the fact that he'd destroyed a stadium with football-shaped bombs, Asinine would wonder how he rose to power.

"If I may be so italicized, I propose *this*." He stabbed the air with a finger. "I would like our seven crime families, the seven largest in this galaxy, to merge into one." He cocked his head at Lieutenant IQ 23. "How am I doing, Lieutenant?"

"Excellent, sir, but the expression is 'be so bold.'"

"A man can be both. And superscripted, too. My posture okay?"

"Great. Those instructional videos really helped." In his white-and-gray plastic armor, IQ 23 smiled and gave a thumbs-up. The head-sized question marks at the temples of his headgear bobbled.

Master Asinine turned back to the others. "How's my plan sound?"

"It sounds crazy!" Grestlix snapped forward in her chair. "Have you gone mad?"

"Only slightly! But maybe this is so crazy it *just— might—work*…even though things rarely work out that way.

"Think about it! The police, Intergalactic Protection, your mothers-in-law. They can all wipe us out easily as it stands right now. Even Grestlix, who is as merciless as gonorrhea, was stopped rather easily at last week's flea market raid."

Grestlix yanked at her short-cut hair. "It's called a stock market invasion, you mindless brute!"

"But imagine if we united. Our power, our control. We won't have to worry about these stupid territorial disputes or useless skirmishes. We'll wipe out the smaller crime families. Together, we'll be so indestructible that no one will destroy us. Not even my old friend, Matross Legion, stands a chance. And we'll work under the thin guise of a business so unlike crime, it's as ironic as a man being beaten to death by his own detached arm. Which reminds me: happy birthday, Requiston."

"You're going at this totally unprepared!" Markiset almost launched out of her chair, her fuchsia Haralsian skin reflecting in the light. "That isn't ironic, you're using grotesque comparisons, and you're being redundant."

"Am I really? Or am I just being so repetitive as to only *appear* to be redundant?" Master Asinine high-fived IQ 23. "Comeback, dispatched." To Markiset, he said, "This idea is so perfect, it's almost as good as Girl Pop Grenade's newest album."

Grestlix covered her ears and sneered at the nearby speaker that played the album. "Newest? It is seven thousand years old."

"And yet still the newest. It's catchy like a plague." Asinine bopped to the beat, menacing them with his angry-chicken head strut. "Anyway, I've thought this plan through. We can pool our resources, weapons, manpower, collections of *Cosmonaut Chimp* comic books. You see, Renovodomus isn't crazy bonkers enough. It's boring. No overabundance of gadgets, no market saturation of doodads. It'll be our job to take over Renovodomus and grace it with enough mad cool stuff to choke the tedium out of it.

"We'll work together instead of apart. We'll function as a business, perform transactions, buy and sell acquisitions, share earnings as if salaried, relocate to an undisclosed party base, and hold rampant, all-night company picnics. We'll operate with the efficiency and power of an organized corporation yet with the lack of conscience of a seal clubber. No law enforcement agency or military will match us. We'll have the resources to barter for the things we need to conquer Renovodomus, and if we can't barter for those things, we'll have the power to take them. This is no matter, though, since we'll make a lot of these." He tossed a few moolah tablets on the table. Currency symbols cha-chinged over his eyes. "Man, I love myself."

Grestlix scrutinized the transparent, blue-glowing tablets. What? No cha-ching? The Houdin leader flicked a tablet away. "Money went electronic centuries ago, caveman. We use thumbprints to transact, remember? And use higher denominations. Five-moolah tablets don't impress anybody."

"From where shall we launch our operations?" Requiston asked.

Asinine forgot the money. "We'll use this great *Mikazin Starship* as our headquarters because it has the funniest bumper stickers. And we'll come up with flashy media names for ourselves. I, my bodyguard, and my lieutenant are now Master Asinine, Braindead, and my lieutenant."

"Braindead?" Wiltroh tried the word out on his mouth, looking as if it tasted like spoiled fish.

"Yes, Braindead. All one word, because he's all one type of special."

Wiltroh chortled. His gray Logistican flab poured off his weakening chair. He shoved a slice of lard cake into his mouth. "That media name is unsound for those who wish to spread fear."

"Those media names sound like Scrabble mishaps," Grestlix said.

"We've been playing with a random insult generator." Lieutenant IQ 23's voice perked. "Braindead's media name was longer, but we cut it down when we found out no one knew what a slackened blow-chunk was."

"And don't forget my name." Master Asinine beamed a smile so wide he let it be his umbrella. "Someone gave me that prestigious title—"

"I'm unconditionally positive it wasn't a compliment," Grestlix said.

"—because I'm the master of the asinine. We've also come up with a secret handshake. We'll show you later. Right now, we will engage in a short Q-and-A session."

Requiston scoffed and searched the faces of the other leaders. His high-pitched Gharalgian voice tittered, scratching fingernails against the chalkboard in Asinine's brain. "So what is your proposed plan to eliminate these other crime families? Shall we simply lay waste to them, annihilating their resources and murdering their underlings?"

"If, by that, you mean demolishing their headquarters, then no. Instead we'll simply lay waste to them, annihilating their resources and murdering their underlings."

"And where have you been lately?" Requiston launched forward in his chair. "As a criminal leader, you've been missing for quite some months. We've seldom heard of you other than incidental skirmishes in locations that barely matter. You went off the grid!"

"Biding my time. Gathering resources. Catching up on my soaps."

"And what is with your atrocious garb?" Grestlix averted her eyes from Master Asinine's outfit. "It blinds even the healthiest of people!"

Master Asinine puffed his chest forward. "Homemade and tailored. Be threatened by its color coordination."

"This sounds suspiciously like your plot to rule the universe using a pickle-powered time machine," Markiset said. "Will this be another doomed failure at which we can laugh from afar?"

"No. You'll join me as partners. You can laugh from anear!"

"This is why you deserted Intergalactic Protection? This is what your disavowal of the military has led to?" Grestlix stood and bumped Asinine back.

"I told them." Asinine stepped forward and sized up Grestlix. Ire churned behind each heavy exhalation. "They abused me, stuffed me into the bottom of the social chain for far too long. Nobody beats me down, least of all the people beating me down."

Requiston grunted in his helium-sucking voice. "And what would we call this amalgamated clan?"

"Ha. This is the best part. We will be…the Bad Guys!" He outstretched his arms and surveyed his visitors. "Eh? Eh? Clever?"

"The Bad Guys?" Wiltroh said. Asinine considered giving him a treadmill. The tub of blubber looked as if nine or ten of his chins would jiggle off whenever he spoke. "What does that mean?"

"The Bad Guys. It's an old Terran expression. *Bad*, defined as 'faulty, unfavorable, worthless.' *Guy*, defined as 'a male, usually Terran.'"

"So we would be worthless male Terrans?" Wiltroh asked. Beside him, Sikth'nkphth hissed, his Virillian forked tongue hanging lazily from his scaly lips.

Master Asinine repeated the expression in his brain, lips moving as he did. "No. Not quite." He shook his head to clear the thought. "Look, just trust me on this."

"What if we *don't* trust you? What happens if we don't want to join?" Grestlix slammed a fist onto the table. Convenient Victim shrieked and threw his arms in front of his face. His teal Trioxidillian skin rippled with a twitching gasp. Heh. Convenient Victim. Master Asinine inwardly scoffed at that name as he had so many times before. He wasn't about to tell the gutless wonder what the English translation meant.

Master Asinine craned his neck forward. "What will happen if you refuse my offer? I've planned for that. I know this proposition intrigues you all. I can tell by your completely indecipherable poker faces. Hypothetically, we will destroy those who refuse to join us in our mad quest for domination. Same with the smaller, more inconsequential crime gangs not represented here today.

"By refusing to join, you become a liability. And we will deal with liabilities…decisively." Asinine reached into his holster and displayed the weapon it gave up with a leathery squeak. "Ladies, gentlemen, and Wiltroh, this is my newest crowd pleaser, the Face Blitzkrieg, cobbled together from bits and pieces I picked up at the thing store." He shifted in a semicircle to display it to everyone. "It was formerly called the Cake Baker until my lieutenant reminded me it doesn't bake cakes. Shame, since Wiltroh and I could really go for a slice right about now."

Wiltroh stammered over his words before producing, "How did you—"

"And that spectacle of technology will do *what* to a target's face?" Grestlix asked.

"With the click of the trigger, whoever you aim at will find out what it's like to have their face blitzkrieged off in painful agony. And that's not all. My tech department is right now working on a satellite superlaser. If the masses don't submit to our new order, we will blitzkrieg the faces off everybody in Renovodomus, one planet at a time. Imagine blitzkrieg on a level bordering on interplanetary."

Asinine studied the crowd from one end of the table to the other. "Everyone, with the four-day, low-carb plan for domination I stole from this month's issue of *Megalomaniac*, we will own crime in Renovodomus. And, with crime, we will own Renovodomus itself." He didn't mention his secret weapon. Not even these leaders would be privy to that. He laughed in his head at their ignorance.

"Four days, everyone. Do we have a deal?" He let those words sink into the resulting silence. His visitors had been snagged like elephants on hooks. Or did the idiom say it was a fish? Whatever. His new electrified nets could fry both those animals.

CHAPTER TWO
A SPOT OF TROUBLE

"Control, acknowledge. Close viewscreen." Major Matross Legion of Intergalactic Protection watched his viewscreen shrink to a dot to conclude his brief conversation with Colonel Patton. Patton had summoned him to his office. What had caused the hint of urgency in Patton's voice? Legion hoped it wasn't another explosion at the celluloid farm. Those missions weren't merciful on his gag reflex.

He squeezed the Alaphan cross on his necklace for comfort, and his fingertip found the bump that marred it thanks to a bullet deflection. He relaxed. Alaphus, his god, always soothed him. He looked at the ceiling, whispered a prayer, and caught sight of the two antennae that sprouted from his skin-covered ears. And the speckle marks from the laser pens he kept tossing up there out of boredom.

Legion wiped the sweat from his face. The deep green skin of his hand found its way to his withdrawn nostrils where a nose would sit on members of most other species.

Wait. His chair! Made from latent technology, it would deactivate once he stood. And he had sat down on this chair absentmindedly. He was so used to nonlatent furniture, but he had recently been forced to change offices to one using l-tech to make way for a higher-ranking officer. Stupid seniority. Some hotshot general had inherited his favorite light panel. And all his cupholders.

L-tech…what an abomination. A technology that deconstructed objects into particles. That arrangement of particles was then stored in computer memory and reconstructed when a user requested. No thanks. L-tech memory was easily corruptible. A more dangerous creation didn't exist. Why, *why* was the technology so popular and trusted? Malfunctioning was its nature, and its memory corruptions could mix, corrode, or misshape objects. Legion didn't want to sit on a misshapen l-chair, but his requests for transfer to an office free of l-tech had gone unheeded.

He gripped the chair's arms with the round pads of his fingertips tight on the wood. A tingle wormed through his limbs. Why must he fight through this fear every time he stood? Because he was paranoid, that was why. Didn't help that one of l-tech's manufacturers was named Explosive Data Diarrhea or that one of its products actually exploded in a bathroom at an irritable bowel syndrome sufferer's meeting. Irony was a force of nature.

He issued a single deep breath—and whipped out of his seat, pressing his forearms against his face as the chair's molecules eddied into the air. The chair disintegrated into its intangible state, and a holographic outline replaced its form to indicate its location and—

And nothing. Fine. But that was the last time he'd sit on that chair. Soon, Alaphus would send an angel to rid the universe of that techno-garbage. While the angel was at it, maybe he could iron a few of Legion's shirts, too.

He exited his office, glad he had no l-door in place (thankfully someone had fulfilled *that* request). He filed through the corridor that led to Patton's office and tightly saluted the soldiers he passed. And one or two shark jugglers.

He passed the base's Letchtech Cryofoods food court where the foul odors of Space Cow's burgers repulsed his nostrils. Over the food court's noise, a public address speaker blared another sponsor advertisement: "Dear warmongers, Dr. Quantum is offering free nanotech liposuction with the purchase of a value-pack facelift deal. Offer valid while supplies last."

The speaker continued, "Intergalactic Protection, Stratus Cloud's military enforcement organization, monitors defense relations between other galaxies and this one—thus the *inter* in *intergalactic*. Since our inception, we have stopped more terrorist acts than any other military agency. We have saved over half the galaxy's planets from destruction. Our Intergalacticnet site yields over twenty million hits per week. Intergalactic Protection, the choice of a new authoritarian rule."

Legion reached Patton's office—and then stopped in midstep. Ugh. The flashy "Letchtech Inside" insignia with its surrounding swirl adorned the door. Patton's office used l-tech. Legion had thought he'd memorized the locations of all the l-doors at Intergalactic Protection. How could he forget one? Was this a low-grade model? A heat flash enveloped his body like a heavy blanket. Or that might have been the heavy blanket a hallway peddler threw over him. No, he didn't want two for a moolah, thanks.

Calm, stay calm. He wrestled out of the blanket, stepped forward—didn't want the door to explode—and knocked.

"Control, acknowledge. Unlock closest door," a voice spoke from the office.

Legion clenched up. He heard the descending *whoomp* of the fading l-door, that ludicrous bane of technology. *Please, please, please, don't kill me.*

No explosion.

In the office, Patton looked up from behind his oak desk, his thick, silvery moustache tweezed between two fingers. Legion wiped sweat from his hairless head and tried to show a demeanor worthy of his position. He squirmed across the threshold of the doorway and into the office…

And the door appeared without incident. Phew.

Patton stood and saluted firmly with a weathered hand. Legion returned the salute. Both released their stances.

"Major Legion, please sit." Patton indicated the outline of an intangible l-chair in front of the desk.

"Yes, sir." Legion shut his eyes tightly and shuffled to the l-chair's outline. He heard the accursed bubbling of the swirl of molecules that collected and hardened into…just a chair. Good. An ugly one, though.

Patton stood behind the desk, still indicating the l-chairs on Legion's side, one chair in its tangible state and one in its intangible state. Legion sat on the tangible one.

It had been a while since he'd visited Patton's office. Awards overpopulated an l-shelf on the office's right wall, displaying Patton's countless accomplishments. And Patton deserved each one, even the one for Most Valuable Player, Foosball Tournament 9099.

A framed image still sat on his desk. Legion looked at it and recognized a younger Patton and the then director of Intergalactic Protection. Their hands were clapped over each other's shoulders, and they cheerfully saluted the camera with their free hands.

Patton dropped into his seat and huffed. An honorable Terran, he had weakened and wrinkled with age, and now his slight girth heaved forward in a troubled slouch. His droop hid the vigor of his broad shoulders and physique, although Legion still spotted the strength concealed beneath that slouch. The many badges of rank and valor on his uniform's left breast jingled as an indication of his decades of experience. Legion hoped to someday become half the hero Patton was. And half the foosball player.

"Before we start, my orders are to tell you the new season of *Full-Contact Car Tag* debuts Monday. Eh. I'm not a big fan of romantic dramas." Patton twirled one end of his moustache between two fingers. "All right, with that out of the way, let's get to business. I can tell you're uneasy, but relax. You aren't in trouble." He smiled, but the rest of his downcast face revealed that his smile was forced.

"I have disturbing news," Patton said. His moustache stretched when he curled the left side of his mouth. Disturbing news? Was he a woman?

Patton stopped twirling his moustache and planted his hands on the desk, fingers intertwined. Only a moment passed before one of those hands found its way back to his moustache. He looked down at his other hand. Under it was a paper-thin computer, a datasheet, that must have contained Legion's mission briefing. "You won't like this, but your old friend, ex-Corporal George Lowensland, is forming a criminal alliance. And, this time, it doesn't look like a ploy to weasel his way into more free cooking lessons."

"Lowensland is back?" That name burned a hole through Legion's brain. He felt his pulse all over his body. "I haven't heard from that monster in months. What's he done now? Is he trying to get those bulls to play tag in the china shop? He's not good at distinguishing between metaphor and reality."

"He now calls himself Master Asinine. I don't think he put the two words together in his head." Patton nodded the thought away. "Reportedly, he cycled through a few names: Baron Boom, Doctor Tragedy, Major Weakling—"

"Major?"

"Yes. He promoted himself by several ranks. What's

stupider is he nominated his subordinate as his lieutenant, apparently as in his lieutenant colonel, not his first lieutenant. Doesn't that idiot remember major ranks below lieutenant colonel? And his 'lieutenant' was never even in the military. Honest. You can't even buy stupidity at that level."

"Once while he was asleep, I put a slice of bread on his forehead and came back five minutes later to burned toast. Let's just be glad he can't prescribe drugs."

"Anyway, this information came to us from an offended criminal leader he passed over when forming his alliance. Anonymous tip."

Years ago, Legion and Lowensland had been squadmates, friends until *that* day, the day he revealed himself as a turncoat, a murderer, a vile blight on society. And Legion still had trouble sleeping at night, knowing someone had amassed as many teen pop albums as that tyrant had.

Legion and Lowensland had been inseparable friends before things had changed. Legion was one of the only two friends Lowensland could claim. Everyone else ridiculed him for his absurdity, his stupidity, his fashion sense. Legion, however, treated him like a brother. They had served together in Intergalactic Protection until Lowensland joined the underside of the law almost six years ago. He formed the Mikazin clan—and killed the third member of their indivisible trio, Sopher. Now Lowensland ranked among society's vilest and most illiterate enemies. And among Legion's, as well. Never had there been a worse corporal than that psycho

Lowensland. His intelligence was a close match to a starship compressor's.

Legion pounded the desk, the l-chair and the l-door almost forgotten. What alliance was Lowensland scheming? He squeezed his paling knuckles so hard they could form diamonds from coal. He wished he had Lowensland's neck in the ripples of those clenched fingers. This was the man who pled court cases by challenging the judges to games of air hockey.

Something was just not right with him.

Patton said, "Major, I know how you feel about Lowensland—"

"They had to update medical waste laws because of him." Legion clearly remembered the circumstances surrounding Lowensland's betrayal, the betrayal Legion should have seen coming. He pictured Sopher's limp body striking the ground, dead from a single fatal gunshot. That gunshot—sounding like a popped balloon—rang through Legion's head right now the same way it did whenever he closed his eyes.

Patton frowned. "Have you been using the anger techniques your therapist gave you? Go over the incident again with me." When Legion grimaced, Patton said, "It helps."

Legion looked at the ground. Was that what the therapy sessions were for? How would he know? He'd never gone to them, and he'd paid someone to fudge his attendance records. If his superiors found out, they'd nail him to the wall. A serious discharge. But he couldn't—*wouldn't*—let therapy expunge Sopher's sacrifice from his mind.

He did his best to recite what a therapist would have taught him to recite. "Sopher and I heard a claxon from IP's primary hangar. Sopher reached the hangar first. I was supposed to arrive with him. Instead I'd returned to my quarters to grab the sidearm I'd forgotten.

"I heard a gunshot when I reached the hangar. I saw a body fall from the boarding ramp of a starship transport. An officer lay dead from a gunshot wound and a cracked skull." His words stiffened. "The dead officer was Sopher. Lowensland had shot him. And I arrived to see him ram his stolen starship through the hangar doors because he never figured out the door opener." He waved his hands angrily. "It has literally only one button!"

"Continue, Major."

Legion sighed. "He escaped with top-secret documents and sold those documents to finance his clan. He endangered everything." Legion pounded his chest. "I should have been prepared. I should have had my sidearm. I promised that day to never lose another friend." Legion didn't mention how Sopher's death was his responsibility, didn't mention the guilt Lowensland left him to suffer alone. This was how Lowensland repaid friendship. "The signed note he left was unnecessary."

"Major, you need to stop beating yourself up. It wasn't your fault, and neither was Lowensland's betrayal. You'll have to put those feelings aside. Control your resentment, or it will jeopardize everyone."

"Everyone ridiculed Lowensland. They all pushed him around, and his only friends were Sopher and me. We should have known better than anyone. *I* should have known. He kept spouting about no longer being everyone's punching bag, kept ranting. Angrier and angrier and *angrier* every time. He said he wasn't taking it any longer. All the signs were there and I never saw them. Wasn't my fault? It was *entirely* my fault!"

Still, the recitation abated the toxic blood in his hairless body. Patton must have seen this because he continued reporting the bad news. "Lowensland's alliance will unite seven crime families into one huge amalgamation. He wants to remake the galaxy in his image, make it 'cooler,' which probably means a tire fire at every key landmark. Major, I won't sugarcoat the magnitude of this. Lowensland's alliance will permanently cripple Renovodomus unless we act now. Their success means we'll kiss order and justice good-bye. I don't know if you've been checking the statistics."

"Religiously, sir. My mind is always on the balance."

"That's good to hear. So you know the ratio of gang members to Intergalactic Protection soldiers is over seventeen to one and getting worse. This only includes the gangs Lowensland has invited. Somehow, we've managed to pull through, but only with each gang working alone. They fought one another as often as they fought us. Their mutual enmity was to our advantage. That and our low, low bagel-stand prices."

"Don't worry. Alaphus will protect us." Would He? Legion found it difficult to believe Patton wouldn't worry when he himself did. For all of Legion's belief in Alaphus, for all of his trust, was his faith nothing when things came down to the crunch? Why was he worrying when Alaphus would protect him? "Alaphus always protects," he said in spite of himself.

"Major, not everyone believes that. I admire your faith, but the higher-ups are looking for a better weapon right now than prayer." Patton began curling the other side of his moustache. "Anyhow, Lowensland has pitched his sale. He's persuaded these gangs to work in tandem, to use that titan-class *Mikazin Starship* as their headquarters. They're now one big family with Lowensland as dear old Daddy. We're outnumbered, outgunned, and outwitted." He reconsidered his statement. "Okay, Lowensland is leading things, but we're still outnumbered and outgunned. Maybe outdrunk, too."

Dear old Daddy. Even a joke about Lowensland as a dad sounded sickening. He'd use landmines to play catch with his kids. "Which gangs has he persuaded?"

"The biggest of the biggest. The information is all stored in this." He motioned to the red datasheet in his hand. The light shimmered off its clear plastic. "The Watercrest clan alone almost wiped us out a few years ago. But all seven together is a step in the right direction for them. He's now commanding thousands of criminals. *Thousands.* We're told, with his new manpower, he'll have Renovodomus in four days, and then Stratus Cloud in a week."

"Four d-days?" Legion's jaw hung open.

"Yes, he can think that far ahead. Major, Renovodomus has one hope for survival." Patton emphasized the statement with his eyes.

Legion sat back. Huh? Why was he here? Was he to play infiltrator on this? Scout? Celebrity stalker? "Sir, what does this have to do with me?"

"Major, the reason I have you here is we're devising a new force that includes untrained civilians. You've been chosen to lead that force. Field Marshal Hullinger handpicked you himself."

"Lead the task force that will beat down Lowensland?" Legion's stomach rippled, and his heart beat so palpably he smelled battery acid. He stood and bobbed on a foot. Then sat. How early could he start? "I accept. I'll take that degenerate down. I might finally get my hedge trimmer back while I'm at it, too."

"Good. You're the only one who knows him well enough. And Field Marshal Hullinger thinks this might give you the closure you need. You *can* command this team. People trust you. They like you. You have a nice singing voice."

"First of all, Field Marshal Hullinger owns the galaxy's largest collection of decorative throw pillows. Do we seriously trust his opinion? Second of all, untrained civilians, sir? Why not use agents from IP?"

"Not that simple. With Lowensland's new army, we'll

need hyperabilities on our side, and we're saddled with the Hyperability Injunction. Nasty legislation. The gangs Lowensland has contacted are composed of criminals with more hyperabilities than we have listed in our database. He probably collected those hyperpeople because of his love of comic superheroes. And the Hyperability Injunction is preventing us from enlisting hyperpeople."

The Hyperability Injunction was enacted thanks to an overenthusiastic and destructive use of a soldier's hyperability at wartime. It led to an intergalactic incident, and sponsors bending to political pressure forced IP to dismiss all hyperpeople. Some pretended to know that the incident was caused by hyperability poisoning, whatever that was. But no one really knew. An error-prone bureaucrat had accidentally expunged its case from history. Some computer operators should be required to have licenses and, if pressed, brains.

Patton continued, "So we have to create a new force and allow hyperpeople to join. It may be sidestepping the injunction and will raise more than a few angry fists, but it's faster than uprooting unanimously voted rulings. And, right now, we don't have the time.

"We already have our eyes on thirty civilians, and you can select seven from them. Most are raw, untrained, unpracticed in anything but the basic use of their hyperabilities. You'll be taking these civilians—if they want to join—and training them yourself, with a little help from us and something I like to call a training montage."

"Montages only work in movies."

"I know, but don't tell Montage Massacre. They sponsor a good chunk of our funding."

"But, sir, I'm Trioxidillian. Next to Fleesons, our race has the smallest occurrence rate of hyperpeople in all humankind. We don't have as much experience with them as Terrans do. I don't know anything about the subject, except that the kid next door to my mom urinates acid in her garden from eight miles in the air."

"Not much to know. Intergalactic Protection will be sending you some information soon. Just learn the terminology and don't collect either of the two illegal combinations of hyperpeople: those who control the four elements and those who control the four fundamental forces. That's about it. Oh, and watch out for hyperability poisoning." Patton handed Legion the briefing datasheet. Legion took it, yearning to crush it in his hands. He peered down at the datasheet, through it, as if his stare could bypass its security lock. Lowensland, that despicable creature, would pay.

Patton tapped his desk. "There are names, addresses, profiles, descriptions, and pictures in that datasheet. You have an eclectic bunch of hyperpeople: people with hyperabilities, people with hypermutations—"

"Hypermutations?"

Patton looked up. "Yes. Hypermutation. It's a…uhhh… hyperability that manifests as a physical mutation. Anyway, you have a communications expert, a telepath, an eel trainer. I could go on. All our resources are yours. A combination space station/shopping mecca is being constructed as we speak. It'll even have a deployable bomb shelter near its core!" Patton shrugged. "And if this thing drags out longer than four days, the station will act as your permanent headquarters. It should be completed in a year. Until then, we're offering you an entire wing of this facility, complete with a great set of training equipment and lockers, some of which don't hide dead rodents. You can activate the datasheet now."

Legion stabbed his thumb over the maroon square in the datasheet's upper-left corner. The datasheet activated with the sound of a brief harp chord, and its transparency clouded to white. It became rigid though it remained as paper-thin as before. First an ad for Silicon Travel—the safest way to travel by cannon—splashed across its surface, but soon a menu screen replaced the ad. Legion jabbed the first option: MISSION BRIEFING. The mission details brushed across the datasheet's display. Legion scanned with his finger as much as with his eyes before mashing his thumb over the datasheet's OFF icon. The datasheet returned to its previous shade of red, drooping like before.

"Seven against thousands." Legion curled the datasheet in his hand. "We'll be overwhelmed. What funding do I have?"

An apologetic curve appeared on Patton's lips. "You'll operate under Intergalactic Protection's sponsorship umbrella, so you'll have mostly Letchtech's funding. They're pushing their new line of mechanical shower caps and they insist you use those products in public. You can refuse it if you want, but you'll have to find your own funding, and you can't get banana-flavored peanut butter anywhere else. Don't go with crunchy. It's a little weird."

"Advertising? To overpower Lowensland? Is there no other way to scrounge up money?" Where were those angels of Alaphus? "Maybe a talent show?"

"You can blame this on crooked politicians looking for reelection." Patton gestured to the Sport Chug ad wiping across a wall. One of Intergalactic Protection's other sponsors. "I'm with you. Just because we need funding from nongovernment entities to avoid political interference doesn't mean we should become slaves to advertisers. But the higher-ups don't agree. I wish we could drop a few sponsors myself, but we have no other income, and I like Bakery Bloodbath's gratuity cookies."

Legion covered the emblem that stretched along his sleeve. Did this mean he could tear the Great Paintballs of Fire logo off his uniform?

Patton snapped to attention. Legion shot to his own feet, crimson thoughts of Lowensland storming him. He saluted so sharply he could have chopped off his head. Patton returned the salute.

"Congratulations, Major Legion. Or should I now call you Lieutenant Colonel?" Patton's moustache curled with a slight smile, and his saluting hand lowered to meet that moustache for another curl.

Legion looked down at the datasheet wrapped tightly in his sweaty grip. He sneered. "Thank you, sir. Lowensland is as good as gone, and that hedge trimmer will be mine."

"You don't even have hedges."

"It's a matter of principle."

CHAPTER THREE
ALMOST AS INTELLIGENT AS YOUR
AVERAGE BLOODSTAIN

"You see," Master Asinine said after he sat on the display counter beside a cash register and set his Face Blitzkrieg aside, "we used to be the McKazin clan, with an *m* and a *c*. I named us after my favorite brand of wall. Simple enough, but when we'd made a name for ourselves, we started receiving food orders every other hour. Nowadays everybody assumes that if your name starts with *Mc*, you're in the food business. We didn't mind until people started coming into our starship and complaining they weren't getting enough special sauce. But we clearly stated *only the McKazin Deluxe* has the special sauce. People still didn't get it. So we changed the spelling of the name to *Mikazin*." He emphasized the first syllable.

The astonished clerk to whom Asinine spoke gawked at the spectacle before him: Lieutenant IQ 23, Braindead, and the other leaders of the Bad Guys rampaging through an electronics store, equipped with baseball bats, traipsing around disarrayed shelves and over small gadgets to reach the really awesome stuff in the back, like that futon that literally ate change. What would drunk science nerds think of next?

Now a mess of broken hardware and appliances, the store contained two shelving l-racks along its narrow display area. The l-racks had been emptied, their contents littering the floor. Similarly, the wall l-racks were empty of all but a few products. Now the small crew of Bad Guy coconspirators and their top-ranking subordinates demolished anything within batting range.

The clamor of sweet destruction had raged mightily but had tapered off now that much of the store's inventory was demolished. Still pelting the silence, though, was the occasional shatter of machinery. And there was Wiltroh, laying ruin to a display of light panels. The sounds of exploding glass and plastic erupted at every strike. That guy was humongous, but boy could he dish out the smackdown on a display model. Convenient Victim cringed in the farthest corner of the store, flinging his arms and tail over his face every time the crack of a bat crushed a hard drive. He clutched his Face Blitzkrieg tenaciously.

"Hey." Master Asinine leaned forward when the clerk didn't respond. "Are you even listening?"

Grestlix approached from behind. She strode over the damaged debris of the store's inventory, probably in search of shinier stuff to break. She held in one hand her baseball bat, in the other a box containing a mindscanner, which she tossed aside. "Asinine, is this at all constructive? Or useful?"

Master Asinine looked over his shoulder. "Certainly. It's

a team-building exercise. I read somewhere that team-building exercises bring groups closer together. They team-build."

"But—how did you put it?—yes, 'knocking over an electronics store.' This is not part of your four-day plan. Shouldn't we prepare instead? Focus on tasks that, perhaps, have *anything to do* with our new coalition?" Grestlix smashed her bat against a wall.

Master Asinine sensed the anger that sharpened Grestlix's demeanor. That same sharp perception informed him that Grestlix's reddened face and maddened eyes said, "Hey, this woman is miffed." Nothing escaped his keen senses.

"These are fun, and we need more batteries for the coin-operated henchbots. Besides, why prepare? Those IP goons don't stand a chance. We outnumber them one to one."

"Do not underestimate them," Grestlix snarled. "What stupidity you are. Your death would be Christmas come early."

"What's Christmas?"

"It is the day before Boxing Day, you crock."

"Boxing Day Eve has a name?"

"Forget it. Just…" Grestlix raised a finger and growled her words. "We may have joined your amalgamation, Asinine, but only with the expectation of picking up the pieces of your shattered plan after watching you fail. Prove to us this is not a half-cocked scheme or you might find yourself on the uncomfortable end of a revolt." She stepped back, waiting a moment before she dropped her finger. "And change your costume. It's as color-coordinated as a kaleidoscope."

"Check this out, sir. You've been looking for one of these." Lieutenant IQ 23 approached, holding what looked like a robotic puppy. He set the puppy on the clerk's counter and leaned over. His mask's question marks drooped. "Okay, Fido. Speak." The puppy yapped a series of electronic barks. Beaming, Lieutenant IQ 23 outstretched both arms to indicate the toy.

Master Asinine clapped once. "Oh, that's cute. Does it also come as a rabid, twelve-foot hellhound?"

CHAPTER FOUR
MISTRUST AND YOUTHFUL STUPIDITY

The surface of Legion's briefing datasheet glinted in the light. Legion read the detailed profiles of two potential recruits. He could have activated three-dimensional holograms of the recruits, but their descriptions offered enough to identify them. He liked these datasheets more than those undependable briefing l-kits Intergalactic Protection had used years ago. And he was clueless as to why his had kept saying, "You've got mail."

From immediately inside the door of the Fireball military starship he'd flown here, he tossed the datasheet onto a passenger chair and strode down the starship's steep access ramp onto the patchy grass and, judging by what frolicked in the distance, rhino droppings. Exactly who walked their pets here?

He inhaled a deep gulp of a Gaian breeze, smelling the beauty of flowery aromas and the drunkard on the bench a few yards away. Gaia was the only planet in Renovodomus with a natural atmosphere, so Legion always regarded his visits here as treats. Domes contained the populated areas on Renovodomus's other five planets. On this planet, everything was open to clean air and a few mean-spirited birds as the fresh goop on his shoulder attested. Nice aim.

The access ramp retracted into the Fireball's side panel. Legion trotted down the hill that swooped into a dale and then approached the construction site that loomed ahead. Clanking girders swayed in the comfortable breeze of a sunny day where a tractor beam lifted them to workers atop what would become an office complex. Right now, the site bore only the skeleton of the complex. Joists sliced the sky in silhouetted lines and intersected in a towering grid that stretched eight stories high. Shouts, clanging, and jackhammers thundered from all directions.

Burning in the back of Legion's mind was his dwindling timeline. Three days until Lowensland's attack, until that madman remade the galaxy for his own deranged benefit, likely killing everyone. He tightened a fist at the thought of that treacherous dog. But Patton's words echoed in his mind: "Control your resentment, or it will jeopardize everyone." Legion's grip loosened. Fine. He would after he strangled that bird with the remarkably good aim.

Legion had come for Mark and Jeff Abends, two childhood runaways. Mark was slightly older than twenty-one age cycles. Jeff was only sixteen age cycles old. They had run away from abusive parents eight years ago, becoming street beggars. They'd spent years in and out of jail for stealing food to survive. Survival stealing was still a crime in the eyes of some heartless judges, and the brothers' crimes had netted them four months. During their last incarceration, they promised they would no longer steal. They returned to begging until the government offered them money for clothing, food, and shelter. That money was four hundred moolahs. Barely enough. They opened a training gym for hyperpeople, but that folded quickly. Since then, they'd slept in alleyways and malls. Better than the zoo's tiger cage the younger one had tried first.

Legion approached and noticed an l-airfoil along the grid's west side that bore sponsorship logos from several different companies. An advertisement spanned the complex's east side, touting Jalopycraft transports: "Transports with flair and guided missiles."

Legion spotted a nearby Terran—people on the ground were scarce—and approached him, his footsteps shushing on the blemished grass. A hardhat topped the portly Terran. He wore unkempt clothes and had tools hanging from his belt. He tapped a holographic blueprint projected from a contraption that sat on the front hood of a civilian transport. The orange hologram, which showed a wireframe blueprint of the building as it would look at completion, zoomed into the position the man had tapped. Over the hologram, "Friedman Postal Supplies" appeared in huge letters, an automatic firearm shooting through the *o*.

"Excuse me? Are you the foreman?" Legion asked the portly Terran.

The man swaggered around. A nametag on his torn breast pocket identified him as Mickey. The gut identified him as an avid couch potato and snack enthusiast. "Yeah. Whadda you want?"

"I'm with Intergalactic Protection. Lieutenant Colonel Matross Legion." Legion plucked his identification from a hip pouch. He displayed it to Mickey, who studied it before looking up with a snort. Legion pocketed his identification. "I'm looking for Mark and Jeff A—"

"Oh, crock!" Mickey snatched his hardhat and clenched a hand over what little hair remained. "Now they're sendin' youse guys afta Jeff? What's he exploded this time? Whenever one o' youse worms come aroun', we lose him for days. We got a schedule to keep, y' know."

Whoa, whoa. Easy, big guy. Legion stepped back but reasserted himself. "I'm afraid my business with them is as confidential as your bellybutton should be."

"Fine. Okay? Fine!" Mickey kicked his civ-tran and lanced the air with a finger, aiming up without looking. "*Don't* hold 'em up or I'll use ya lungs as water balloons."

"Funny. I get the same threat from my dentist."

"They're workin' on my weldin' on the top floor. Youse can use the l-airfoil to levitate up."

"L-airfoil?" Legion's mouth dried. "You have anything else?"

"The regular airfoil." Mickey tossed a thumb over his shoulder. "But why? L-airfoil's quicker. Regular one's only for emergencies and peein' when ya can't get ta the stall quick enough."

Legion looked to the side of the building. A makeshift airfoil shaft extended to the top floor, and riders used it by stepping on a speckled levitator panel at the bottom of that shaft.

"That's okay. It'll do."

"Whatever floats ya boat."

Legion rushed to the regular airfoil, giving the l-tech one a wide berth. Good. Regular airfoils weren't frightening and unreliable like l-airfoils. He stepped through the door in the airfoil's tube, avoided the yellow splotches, and settled onto the levitator panel. The levitator panel lit up. A gust of wind blew through its speckled holes and made Legion drift upward. He could have commanded the airfoil to quicken his lift, but the eighth floor wasn't too high and he wanted to keep his lunch. And—*sniff*—evidently a lot of people couldn't make it to the stall.

In seconds, he reached the top. For a regular airfoil, the ride was quick but, given that the brothers' hyperabilities could be used for self-propelled flight, Legion would have them bring him down. More convenient. Well, a trip with Mark would be more convenient. Jeff was liable to hurl him into the ground. (The datasheet's words, not Legion's.)

He assessed the top floor. Beams outlined the grid, and floor panels filled the gaps between some of those beams, but not much else was up here. A dozen workers confidently traipsed across the beams like tightrope walkers. Oops. Make that eleven. One guy blundered off and took a five-minute-to-forever breather. A stack of plywood broke his fall and—ugh—his neck. That'd leave a bruise.

Legion stepped off the airfoil and onto a floor panel, and soon his ears flooded again with the sounds of construction. He looked ahead and spotted the brothers in the distance. Jeff was blasting a large plank with a thin bolt of light his index finger emitted. A Virillian approached him from behind.

Jeff apparently had a mental handicap that saddled him with a maturity instability. And his grammar was all over the map thanks to his handicap and a shoddy school system. Apparently he was allergic to consistent sentence structure. A doctor's assessment corroborated the symptoms. Weird.

He projected light from his body into a laser or flew by casting light energy away from himself. So said the information Legion had derived from police intelligence and incident reports at children's birthday parties.

What the briefing datasheet said about Mark was notably different. Mark Abends was more muscular and taller by a few inches. The more mature of the two, he controlled fire in the same way his brother controlled light. An elemental. He wore l-clothing to avoid burning his regular clothing. Dangerous fashion style considering the underwear.

Mark sat on a girder, ignorant of the clank of metal striking metal every two or three seconds. He concentrated on welding two long beams into an L by wrapping their endpoints in a meltproof mold. He heated his palms and, after a few seconds, released the endpoints. He removed the mold. The beams were fused together.

The Virillian left Jeff's side to help a pair of Trioxidillians erect a rectangular structure. Jeff called out to Mark, so Legion stopped. He hoped to convince them quickly—he still had four others from Gaia to persuade—but he spared a few moments to watch them interact.

"Hey, Mark," Jeff hollered, and Mark pivoted to face him. Jeff lifted his shirt to reveal a set of ridges on an emaciated abdomen, his strikingly blond hair shining in the sunlight. "Check it out, Mark, check this out. This *so* awesome. I was uppin' my exercise again. I started growin' some muscle. Ya almost sees a line 'round my six-pack. Well, s'not a six-pack yet. Like a two-pack. Or a backpack. Whatever. It's a BYOB o' muscle bonanza. Ain't it cool?" Jeff traced a line around his abdomen. He looked as if he'd never eaten more than crumbs. Or that ant he just licked off a girder.

"I can't see it," Mark said, his hair so red its color ignited in the daylight.

"Wai-wai-wait." Jeff stepped sideways, out of a shadow. "Maybe the light ain't good. Okay, okay, okay. How's 'bout now? Maybe I should sucks it in a bit." He sipped the air to compress his stomach as much as he could. "Look at dat! You can sees it?"

"Nope."

"Moves back. Ya might gotta moves back a bit. Moves back. Sometimes ya can't sees nothin' unless ya moves back."

Mark chuckled. "I told you, someone with your body type will never grow big muscles. You have slim abs. You'll have to settle for a wiry body no matter what."

Jeff pouted pensively and pinched his stomach. He produced no flab. "Well, s'good thing I gots a met'bolism like a high school geek or I gets a gut maybe, huh."

The Virillian returned and tapped Jeff's shoulder. Jeff gave the Virillian a happy glance, and Mark chuckled again. He resumed his work.

Legion chose this point to approach them. "Mark and Jeff Abends?"

Jeff remained preoccupied with the Virillian, but Mark looked up. His mop of fiery hair drooped shallowly over his forehead.

Mark's red eyes hardened with suspicion. An odd color for Terran eyes. "Yes?" His word sounded like a knife being sharpened. Legion sensed the uneasiness, the distrust. How often had the authorities come for them in exactly this way? Leftover warrants from their thievery days probably often returned hauntingly. To them, trusting people was alien. Convincing these brothers would be tough, but their profiles insisted they would be valuable additions to Legion's lineup, especially if they'd compete against the Logistican pop-and-lock dance troupe.

Mark set the fused L-beam down, his attention focused solely on Legion. Legion approached, so Mark sprang up and backed away. Legion stopped and extended his hand. "I'm

Lieutenant Colonel Matross Legion of Intergalactic Protec—"

"Oh, no." Mark pointed at Legion as if warning him to step away. "What's my brother destroyed this time? A balloon stand? Another pig?"

"What? He hasn't—"

"It's not his fault he's so powerful. He just needs to learn control. He has a disability that keeps his mind from maturing. Will you people get off his case? Level with me. Was it another pig?"

"No, it's not about that! Actually, this concerns both of you." Legion retracted his hand since Mark refused to shake. Mark would probably burn it off, anyway.

"What can this possibly be about?" Mark's words leaked out. He scanned Legion.

Legion stepped forward, but Mark stepped backward, stretching the gap Legion had tried to bridge. "I have an offer for you and your brother."

Mark's face sharpened again. His head leaned to one side. "Jeff, come here please."

"Name's Jeffy!" Jeff looked back to the Virillian. "Sorry, big, ugly, bucktooth troll-gump whats name I can't pronounce. My brotha gotta haves a word wit' me. An' you gots nose hairs what dance when ya breathes. Gross." He stepped around the Virillian, slapped the tall "troll-gump" on the back of the shoulder, and bounced forward. Virillians were disagreeable and, though to a Terran a slap on the back meant camaraderie, to a Virillian it meant disrespect. This Virillian growled openmouthed at Jeff. Most Virillians couldn't make sounds, but others uttered only growls and roars. This Virillian belonged to the verbal kind: noisy and unpleasant. And, given the stench blowing in the wind, thoroughly stinky.

"What th' big mishap, Mark?" Jeff bounded to Mark and then noticed Legion. "Who you? You here an' tells us we gotta moves outta our cardboard box? I only go if me an' Mark gets lollipops."

Legion scrutinized Jeff. "You two live in a cardboard box?"

"Yeah, a really fierce fridge doojigger box. I drew a flowers bed on it."

"Look, let's skip the discussion about our living arrangements and my brother's idea that any garden he draws with a cutting torch will come to life. Get on with your offer." Mark stepped in front of Jeff to block Legion's view of him. Legion felt a wave of heat push him back. Had Mark's anger actually manifested heat?

Okay, these two seemed unstable. One reacted with more hot blood than a gambling addict losing a hand of blackjack, and the other had the common sense of a rock. And had just poked himself in the eye. But they were powerful and, thus, valuable.

Legion sidestepped to view Jeff as well as Mark. "I represent Intergalactic Protection, and I'm not sure if you've heard of George Lowensland and the Mikazin clan—"

"Yeah, I've heard of them." Mark crossed his arms and

began tapping his foot. "What about them?"

"Lowensland has merged the seven largest crime families in Renovodomus into one super family."

"A über fam'ly." Jeff raised an eyebrow at Mark. "*Über.* Been waitin' weeks to use dat word. It sound real fierce, huh." He thrust his arm enthusiastically at Legion. "We gotta joins wit' this guy, ya know. Come on, Mark. We can flies those way awesome tran'ports and be all like *woohoo* wit' them impact suits and we takes nothin' from nobody all like we big an' mean—"

Mark eased a hand onto Jeff's shoulder to calm him. Wow. The gesture worked. "Jeff, settle down. The last time you got this overexcited, you threw up all over the arresting officer."

"Name's Jeffy," Jeff said. He sneezed, faltered back, and put a finger under his nose. "Whoa. Did I talks all good grammar just now?"

Legion exhaled. "Anyway, what these crime families have together is a formidable force. Alone, any one of them doesn't stand a chance. But now they're together"—to signify a union, Legion joined his hands into a mishmash of fingers—"so they outnumber us. And we have three more days to tip the odds in our favor or else Lowensland launches a powerful attack we don't have the manpower or sneeze guards to counter. His plan is to tear down everything our society stands for and remodel it to his gain. He's so unstable that taking over the galaxy likely means killing everyone in it. The teen pop music alone…" Legion shivered. "By the way, someone's walking a rhino down there." He pointed to the field. "What kind of leash laws can you guys *not* break around here?"

A worker passed by. She cleared her throat and spat out a slimy wad of phlegm. Legion's abdomen tied a knot that forced his lunch to churn.

"So you cames 'cause you Intergalsnatchup Protactaloid guys gonna get the tender parts o' your butts über up?" Jeff asked.

Legion swallowed down the knot in his stomach. "Yes. I mean no—"

"You mean yes," Mark said.

"Well…yes. Everybody will get their butts übered up. Look, let's stop using *über* as a verb in relation to butts. It's downright disturbing." Legion bit his lower lip. Jeff and Mark were still confused. Especially Jeff, and Legion was learning how easy that was. The one with the brains in this pair was obvious. But Jeff's mental deficiency made things simpler for Legion: only Mark needed convincing. Jeff would follow. "Intergalactic Protection is at an incredible loss with this criminal merger. It's against intergalactic treaty for us to hire hyperpeople, and this new merger is mostly composed of hyperpeople who will easily knock us into next week. I'm heading a new team…and that's where you come in."

"So how can you hire us?" Mark's voice edged a notch louder. "We have hyperabilities."

"Since we don't intend to enter a war zone, the

Hyperability Injunction technically doesn't cover us. That's a wartime law. We're just law enforcement. We exist only to stop the Mikazin clan."

Mark considered this, but his expression looked dour. "No. There's no *we* here. We can't quit this job. I'm not risking my brother going hungry because IP thinks it'll be a lark to throw together some fly-by-night task force. We're out."

"What he said." Jeff nodded. "Plus I gonna locks it wit' the black magic."

"That's 'locking it with the golden key,'" Mark said.

"Then I gonna locks it wit' the gold donkey."

Legion shook his head. "No, this isn't a fly-by-night—"

"It solar powered?" Jeff grabbed his brother's collar. "That even so much better, Mark!"

"No, no. Intergalactic Protection is funding us, and IP doesn't run fly-by-night operations. Mark, I understand it's not a good idea for you and your brother to abandon the only job you've been able to hold since Jeff put job listings out as a dental floss expert—really narrow niche, by the way—but… your debts."

Mark's face stiffened, not with anger this time but with suspicion.

"That's right. Mark, your debts. We've calculated them—"

"You accessed my credit record?" Mark stamped forward and emanated another wave of heat.

Legion stepped back and shielded his face, his eyes

teary. "We've calculated your debts, and you have, at best, forty-three more years until they're paid. That's ignoring rising interest and assuming there are no more chicken-farm incidents. We've also calculated your business loan for your gym. Eighteen additional years. That's sixty-one years. Mark, IP is offering to pay them for you. Tomorrow, they'll be wiped clean."

"I still don't like it. It's a no-go. My brother's future comes before some whimsical Intergalactic Protection project. It comes before anything. I need to safeguard him. He still sucks his thumb. Find some other hyperpeople patsies. Jeff, let's get back to work. And stop sucking your thumb." Mark took Jeff's arm gently and stepped away, but Legion jumped in front of him. Mark shot him a glare. His heat slapped Legion with a more intense wave, and the girder under his feet sizzled.

Jeff pulled at his brother's arm. "Mark, but we can flies them really cool transports. Them transports! Gonna be so fierce. Oh, mebbe a starship instead. Them's makes better pet shelter bulldozers." He smiled, his eyes glazing over in daydream. "Watch out, fat gerbil."

"Jeff, a starship is a type of transport. They're just larger and kill more people."

"Like wienie dogs."

Legion said, "Mark, please listen. I promise, absolutely promise—and think about this—your brother…off the streets forever. Out of the criminal element you've worked so hard to keep him from."

"But Criminal Element's my favoritest pizza place ever." Jeff checked his brother. "We still talkin' about wienie dogs?"

Legion continued, "He'll be fed, clothed, educated, sheltered, given friends, given a chance at what was stripped from you both"—Legion gestured at Jeff, who was chewing on caulking—"given a proper diet. You can finally offer him the life you tried so hard to provide but never could. And you could teach him not to chase his own tailbone like he's doing right now."

Mark's face loosened. Jeff's situation was the key to winning him over. Legion thanked Alaphus for His help. He needed Mark and Jeff.

"My brother will have a home?" Mark looked back up and wiped his damp eye.

"Guaranteed."

Jeff examined his brother. "Mark, if ya do that leaky thing outta your eye, s'okay. But if it's come outta your nose, that's gross an' I gonna have to punch you in the head bone."

Mickey scanned the blueprint projectin' from the device on the front hood o' his civ-tran. He tapped it wit' his index finger and it rotated to a sky-blue area: unfinished. The building was progressin' quickly. Nice. Things were even under budget.

Heat brushed his side, the telltale sign o' Mark flyin' down to the ground. Without lookin', Mickey asked, "Mark, youse finished that weldin'?"

"Nuh-uh. We takin' off, big boss foreman man!" Jeff said. He an' Mark passed behind Mickey.

"Off? S'not even…" Mickey checked his watch. Stopped again? He shook his wrist to wake it up. Nanotechnology powered the pissin' thing and it *still* broke.

"He means we're quitting," Mark said.

"Run! That guy's rhino is charging us!" Legion dashed off.

"Jeff, don't moon it!" Mark roared into flight.

Mickey's jaw dropped. Quittin'? He darted around the civ-tran. Jeff, Mark, and that IP guy, leavin'. No! "We'll never finish this stuff under budget wit' youse guys gone. Come back here!" They couldn't hear him. They'd raced across the field and into the IP starship before the rhino could gore them. They was leavin'! "*Come back!*"

The starship blasted off and the whir of its engines faded. Mickey slammed his fist into a nearby girder. "For pissin' sake—" He threw his hardhat at the ground and kicked it away. Now he had no welders.

Okay. Fine. He'd finish this job without 'em. Stuck two fingers in his mouth an' issued a piercin' whistle. "Hey, Lou!"

"Hey, what?" Lou yelled back. He was hauling a pipe on his shoulder, which he rolled off and set on the dirt.

"Them huge green-and-purple robots your cousin knows. They still lookin' for a job?"

"Yeah. Why?"

"Tell 'em the job is theirs so long as I don't have to hear them spew that 'Constructobots, merge into Devastate-it, the most powerful structural engineer' speech every time they punch in."

CHAPTER FIVE
A ONE-SIDED THINK TANK

Behind his desk, Master Asinine looked up from his datasheet—a how-to guide on washing your hands—to see Grestlix enter his office. Grestlix's chief guard, a spiteful two-headed Terran media-named Schizophrenic, followed and stepped aside to stand next to Braindead, who stood on the right of the door in his new gray-and-black impact suit. Lieutenant IQ 23 stood on the other side of the door and watched Grestlix warily. The office's l-door reappeared.

Asinine noticed Schizophrenic's T-shirt. It bore lettering that read "I'm Stupid" under the right head and "I'm With Stupid" under the left, an upward-pointing arrow above each. Asinine didn't get it.

"So?" Grestlix approached the l-chair that Master Asinine's triumphal butt didn't occupy. After the l-chair appeared under her, she shifted forward and faced Asinine from across the landmark piece of furniture in this room: his atomic desk. Or at least that was what Asinine had called it after he'd discovered it could detonate on command. He chortled silently. What a selling feature.

"What is the matter of such urgency for which you

rushed me here?" Grestlix's curling lip and angry stomp, all were signs that she respected Master Asinine as a vast superior. Especially when feasting her eyes on the greatness of the orange-painted color scheme of Asinine's office walls. "I sat down in my cubicle—which, by the way, is utterly ridiculous in a criminal organization—when suddenly plastic streamers, balloons, confetti, and sparklers dropped from my ceiling. Then a shrill noisemaker alarm informed me I was the millionth person to sit in my chair and I should make my way to your office to claim my prize. The commotion would have been enough without the siren in the background."

Master Asinine waved Grestlix's concern off. "Forget that. Big discount at Party Planet. Just my way of enticing you over here, and I had to use that stuff *somewhere*." He leaned forward and said in a clandestine whisper, "An information leak of mine at IP has given us some valuable gossip about a special task force my old cohort, Matross Legion, is leading. It's being created to counter a certain amalgamated crime family."

"And you gathered that crime family is us," Grestlix said.

Master Asinine jerked back—holy crock—and couldn't hide the shock that blasted his face, couldn't squelch the spark that electrocuted his body. "You...you think it's us?" He stood, removed his helmet, and slapped a palm on his forehead. "That's...that's...It probably *is* us. How flattering."

"You mean that hadn't struck you?" Grestlix kicked the

desk. "You deluded, idiotic—Who is this information leak, anyway?"

Master Asinine stood and tossed his arms up. "I never got her name. I just dialed zero one day when I contacted IP's lost-and-found hotline, looking for my favorite pair of needle-nose pliers. I got the receptionist. She's very chatty." He wiped the sweat from his brow and dropped into his seat. "We need a plan, don't we?"

"We certainly do, you ignoramus!"

"No need to trade Latin compliments right now. Now is the time to strike. We make sure they know their days are numbered, that we aim to take over this galaxy. With festive lights and morning shows and stuff. Grestlix, I want you to form a team of six, blast your way into IP, and make some chopped liver. And while you're preparing dinner, see what you can do to wipe out this task force. I want a message delivered: 'Leave Renovodomus because you don't play fair and you can't borrow my action figures.'"

"A team of six? To successfully execute this mission will require an army!"

"We can't spare the snack food for the trip."

"Are you for real? Have you any suggestions on what I use for weaponry?" Grestlix spat a sour laugh. "A water pistol?"

"Even better." Master Asinine opened one of his desk drawers. From it, he produced a contraption about twice the length of his hand: a thick stick that split into two ends halfway down, an elastic band tied between the ends of the split. This he placed on the desk with a *thunk*. "This will be your weapon."

Grestlix stared down at it, her eyebrows raised. "What is it?" Each syllable was stretched.

Asinine shrugged with his hands. "Are you kidding? It's a fling-a-majig. What do you think it is? It flings majigs. Specifically *a* majig. Oh, and here's your majig." He reached into the desk drawer and produced a rock. He set this next to the fling-a-majig. His secret weapon could come in handy on this mission, but he'd save that for his own use.

"These baubles are rubbish. Why would I not use my Face Blitzkrieg?" Grestlix stomped her foot in a sign of definite respect for Asinine. "And which pilot should I take? The narcoleptic, post–nuclear winter psychotic or the blind, hallucinating paraplegic?"

Master Asinine tapped his chin in thought. "The narcoleptic psychotic. Safety first."

Grestlix whipped to her feet. "Fine, but this discussion is far from over."

"Thanks to my uncanny ability to stretch conversations past the point of stupidity," Asinine called out at Grestlix's departing back. The *whoomp* of the l-door's fading punctuated the end of his sentence.

Schizophrenic followed Grestlix in boots large enough to lodge into an elephant's mouth. Brimming with sardonic confidence, he kept, at his left hip, the Face Blitzkrieg he'd been given. Asinine wasn't sure Schizophrenic needed it, though. Sixty workouts a week wouldn't give anyone the intimidation factor this hulk boasted.

"Wait." Master Asinine lifted a hand.

Schizophrenic paused, and the l-door reappeared when he didn't pass. His two heads looked at each other, both sets of their jet-black hair rustling. The dominant left head, Lefty, wore the arrogance of a no-nonsense rebel, a chewed toothpick in his sneering mouth. Righty showed his obtuseness by gaping blankly at the three-dimensional image still behind Asinine.

"Wait for what?" Lefty's eyes became stony. Schizophrenic returned to Asinine's desk and slammed his foot onto it, revealing a tattered, salt-stained pant leg. The desktop computer embedded in the desk complained with a sharp beep. The odor of dirt and mud filtered from him, not overpowering but still noticeable. He seemed unopposed to getting his hands dirty. "What do you want, you wailing monkey pump?"

"Ooh, good one. Anyway…" As if someone could overhear him, Asinine's eyes crawled left to right in a malevolent shift. Or at least he hoped they showed malevolence. That was one of his better expressions. It displayed the fullness of his cheeks. "I have a proposition for you."

"Proposition?" Lefty snorted, Righty still staring at the picture like a drugged crash test dummy. "I'm not like that."

"Wha—No, not a marriage proposition. A business proposition."

Lefty snorted again. Seemed to be his favorite way to begin or end a sentence. "What's this jerk-in-the-box propos—"

"Hey, I see it." Righty pointed at the picture. "It's a sailboat. Neat."

"For crock." Lefty's unshaven chin bobbed and his toothpick shifted. "Look, we're conducting business, you emptied brain. Pluck your head out of our poop crack for thirty to forty seconds a day like we agreed in our contract. A freaking comedy of errors, aren't you?"

"Forget it. Just..." Master Asinine took a moment to breathe. "I propose—"

"I'm still not into—"

"*You*"—Asinine chopped the air with a rigid hand, which he hoped would cut the conversation—"were the chief of security of the Houdin clan before the merger. Now you retain only the mediocre title of head guard. No pun intended."

The heads nodded, Righty nodding no but switching when he noticed Lefty nodding yes.

Asinine looked into Schizophrenic's pairs of eyes. He tented his fingers in front of his nose and drummed them together. "How would you like to join my team, become *my* chief of security?" He let a curt laugh escape him.

"I thought all you guys were on the same team," Lefty

said.

"Not exactly. I just have…a job…for you on Grestlix's mission." The smile on Master Asinine's lips broadened. "Which reminds me: can you pick up toilet paper on the way back? Two-ply because it's cushiony for my tushiony."

CHAPTER SIX
GUIDED TOUR IN THE BLANK ABYSS OF
HOPELESSNESS

"Intergalactic Protection, now with sixteen percent more strategy than Pinky and the Brain use," yakked the haunt control's bloody advertisement program from an overhead speaker that seemed to pick Everett Pendleton out of a crowd and follow him. Just like the advertising jingle sang, haunt controls operated locations, making them seem haunted. That was why they were called haunt controls.

On the gloomy planet of Minerva, Pendleton exited the military transport that had shuttled him to Intergalactic Protection headquarters. He hadn't been on a mil-tran or to Minerva in a year and a half, ever since the Hyperability Injunction was enacted. He bore IP no animosity: those blasted tossers dismissed who they needed to dismiss to maintain intergalactic peace and, frankly, he needed the break from his past and the sodding rations Chicken Carnage inflicted on the troops. With a business name like that, Pendleton was 90 percent sure they stopped using real chicken around the time beaks stopped appearing in their meals.

"Intergalactic Protection, boasting an infantry arsenal fit

for an infant. You'll love our new fighter-jet booster seats."
Wait. When would an infantry use a fighter jet?

Pendleton shook from the gentle wind, his wing feathers ruffling. He immediately recalled the claustrophobic feeling of Minerva's atmospheric domes. Everything shielded under those domes was cold metal, everything outside them desolate rock. Not a vacation spot.

Jacob, that fidgety youth Pendleton had met on the miltran, debarked behind him. The youth whistled when he spotted the skyscraping dome under which they now stood. "Way more impressive than a sports stadium." He, too, was chosen to join this new task force. He'd bragged during the trip here about how he was born to fight. From his days serving in the military, Pendleton knew braggarts frightened the most easily.

"I should hope so. Intergalactic Protection sometimes hosts the dodgeball finals under its domes."

"Intergalactic Protection, your first choice in germ warfare," the haunt control said.

"And sometimes you just want to dodge their blooming advertising campaigns."

Pendleton stretched the hawklike wings that sprouted from his shoulder blades. His hypermutation. After he'd sat in that cramped mil-tran for hours, the stretch felt smashing.

"Intergalactic Protection, brought to you—" Okay, at this point, Pendleton was convinced the haunt control spoke just to hear its own voice.

He faced the vast parking lot dotted with planet-based transports and their larger versions, starships. The scant trees and grass didn't make up for the industrial look of the buildings ahead, even though the mutated talking bushes tried to convince people otherwise. He started toward the doors that led to Intergalactic Protection's main lobby—when a balloon filled with pink paint struck him in the back of the head. There he stood, soaked with paint that leached down his hair and feathers. He examined the splash. Oh, bloody sod. How would he clean this out of his clothes? Dreadful.

A group of enraged women shoved themselves against a wall of soldiers in riot gear. In a litany of curses, their voices thunderstormed: "Chauvinists! Pigs! Chauvinist pigs!" Protestors. And repetitive ones at that.

"You okay?" With a mix of concern and aversion, Jacob studied the paint now dripping from Pendleton.

"Yes. Thank you for asking, mate. It is just paint." Pendleton swept the pink gunk from his shirt and flicked it off his taloned hands. "Industrial paint, but just paint." Tasted like pepper. Oh, and it was toxic. His brain was going to have jolly fun with him this evening.

Years ago, Intergalactic Protection had accepted sponsorship from MaxSport for their male-targeted Sport Chug. MaxSport had pressured Intergalactic Protection into firing all its female soldiers because an all-male military that drank their product boosted sales. If Intergalactic Protection refused to comply, MaxSport would withhold its military funding. Pendleton disagreed with their ethics, but he hadn't sat in the control chair during that advertising meeting. Good thing, too, because Chicken Carnage had catered it.

Smoldering anger surged inside him. No. He stopped, concentrated. He needed to bottle that emotion, prevent it from creeping into his actions. He needed to remain stoic, remain cold, remain detached. No use getting into a row over things. He ignored the protestors and continued toward the lobby. There, he showed identification to the two soldiers who manned the doors. Those soldiers offered samples of crumb cake as per IP's advertising agreement with Gorgeaholic Foods. Jacob grabbed a sample and followed, cracking his knuckles for the hundredth time since the mil-tran had picked them up.

"Jacob, trust me. Refrain from eating that sample."

"But it combines two of my favorite things: crumb cakes and crumbs." Jacob stuffed the sample into his mouth. "Holy gastronomical crock! Who thought cinnamon and jalapeños would go well together?" He pounded his fists on a wall and coughed foggily. "It tastes like a mouthful of used diaper and olive oil. What gives, science?"

"Intergalactic Protection, the choice of a new authoritarian rule. Intergalactic Protection, no longer able to be taken in a high school brawl. Intergalactic Pro—"

Pendleton entered the lobby and scanned for Lieutenant Colonel Matross Legion. Ahead, someone pressed a thumb against the thumbprint reader of a candy machine to pay for a snack. Behind the snack eater stood Legion in the middle of a small crowd that included a young blond who leaped around and hooted as if he'd consumed only caffeine pills.

Jacob writhed on the ground. "It's in my sinuses now. I can't see the color green anymore. Why can't I see green?"

Aha. There was Lieutenant Colonel Legion, that bloke. The lieutenant colonel stood under a light panel, his green skin looking like a lime under the illumination. He addressed those he had collected here with his hands forming a megaphone. "Okay, I just got news that the haunt control is stuck in an infinite loop, so we're going to hear the self-advertisements for a while. The techies have no idea what went wrong, so they're just calling the haunt control Loopy and going with it. Standard fare."

The hooting blond burst into self-propelled flight. Standing under him, a redheaded Terran folded his muscular arms. "Jeff, what have I told you about swinging from chandeliers?"

"Intergalactic Protection, with a new policy reminding you to please stay off our chandeliers."

"And the higher-ups want you to start thinking of media names and outfits so they can market your likenesses into children's toys, lunch boxes, and mountainside landmarks." Legion hushed his voice to something he'd keep to himself even though it needed to be said aloud. "As long as it gets money from l-tech sponsors out of here, I'm all for it."

Legion's tour concluded in a lonely hallway off a dead-end wing of the facility, where he guided his seven new soldiers to the training gym. It stood as the single door in this stretch of dirty corridor. "And this is our training gym, where I'm obliged to tell you Splunge fruit juices contain seventeen essential nanobots programmed to give you an eighty-five percent more efficient lifestyle." He tried not to sound too contrived.

Legion checked the gym, a room furnished with metallic walls and nothing more. The sensation of prickling needles trickled through him when he noticed how little Intergalactic Protection had thus far equipped the basketball court–sized weight room. He studied the faces of those he'd collected. Those faces surveyed the barren gym that held his echoing voice and still smelled of lemon-scented cleanser. The locker rooms to the left had held little more when last Legion had checked, and they probably remained that way now if the cockroaches hadn't moved their belongings in yet. The cardio room was probably as unfurnished.

"Wow." Jeff hung his head into the room. His bones became accentuated in the fatless wire of his neck. "I sees missin' war stuff for miles in here. Where the water cooler?"

"It's in the corner." Silas Reef, their Terran strategist, pointed. "And it's filled with mouse bones. I don't know if it's being used as a garbage container or a warning."

Legion felt his green skin blush to a darker shade. "Well, the training gym isn't exactly complete. Not yet, anyway, since IP still needs to order the equipment, install the gym's software, and put up the motivational posters of kittens hanging from branches."

Jacob Refensil entered the weight room. Wasn't he the Terran who created independent duplicates of himself? Creating each duplicate reportedly gave him headaches. Still, that was a hyperability Legion wished he had in so many situations, especially when facing morning exercise drills. "The gym looks like a linoleum desert!" His voice echoed loudly. His knuckle-cracking echoed even more loudly. Why did his breath smell like bad jalapeños?

"When will it be completed?" Ghiglix, a member of the Fleeson species, asked. He zipped into the room at a supersonic speed. When Legion blinked, he had zipped back out, narrowly missing their Terran computer expert, Aaron Khouri.

Legion reexamined the room's bareness with a deflating mood. "Any day now. I guess."

A pair of hands clutched his collar and yanked him from the group, who still gawked at the room's emptiness. The hands belonged to Mark Abends, who'd been glaring since his arrival. Yeah, this would end well. "Is this what I risked my brother's future for? An empty training gym, a boneyard for a water cooler, and a tour of IP's newest space station? The only reason I agreed to join was to give Jeff a better life and maybe teach him to stop shaving off his eyebrows."

"I guess IP just hasn't filled the gym yet." Legion felt

that same lightheadedness he felt whenever he lied about his therapy attendance.

"Hasn't filled it yet? Well, they'd better fill it. The training gym I owned had more equipment than this." Mark's searing heat flapped against Legion, rich with sizzling intent.

"Incoming intercom connection," the station's haunt control said from a public address speaker nestled in one corner of the hallway.

Legion pulled away from Mark's grip, scorch marks now marring his collar. "Control, acknowledge. Accept connection." He clutched his Alaphan necklace and kept one eye lingering on Mark's angry stare.

"This connection brought to you thanks to Dartman's Pet Interment," the haunt control said. "We don't use pet cemeteries because we don't like supernatural comeuppances."

Legion still watched Mark. "Legion here."

"Patton here." His superior's voice sounded as crisp and as dignified as if they'd stood in the same room. "Lieutenant Colonel Legion, a transport is approaching your area. It's not answering our hailing requests. Can you check—"

A crumbling explosion! The connection disengaged. An enormous spike mashed through a wall and sliced it open to the night of the fake atmosphere outside. Dust and a transport's odor of ozone clouded Legion's nostrils. The spike drilled through to reveal itself as the nose cone of a Lasergem transport. When the starship finished its penetration, its nose cone flipped open.

Hailing request answered, Legion guessed.

No! His soldiers weren't ready. "Everyone, stay behind me. Find cover! Jeff, stop dancing in front of the starship."

Everett yelled over the cacophony of the crumbling wall and the roaring transport engines, "Lieutenant Colonel Legion, mate, I believe you have called us onto your team for a purpose. We need to fight alongside you." He shoved past Jeff. "If some of us would stop capering around in front of the enemy's starship, we could do that."

Legion clenched his hands. Fine. Everett was right. Legion shook at the thought but...yes, they were called here for a purpose, all seven who had accepted out of the thirty names IP had given him. Patton had known what he was doing when he'd suggested these hyperpeople. Please may no one die. No one. "Fine." Legion pulled out his Marsek pistol. "As of now, you're all on duty. This is a Lasergem, and Lasergems only fit six, so...uh...wait." Only six? What idiot drilled into Intergalactic Protection headquarters with a six-man transport? Aside from the IP staff sergeant who liked a little twist in his morning coffee.

Whatever. Legion's soldiers may not be outnumbered but, with no training, they were unquestionably outmatched. "Let's make this a well-executed first fight. Shoot to kill when they emerge. Mark, provide cover fire and take down anyone who comes out. Jeff—"

"Name's Jeffy!"

"—stop making farting noises with your armpit and

flank high. Everett, gun from the front. Aaron, provide fire from a low vantage point. Ghiglix, build an airlock around that hole so the neighbors don't suspect any wild parties. The rest of you, be ready for anything. This might just be that pesky news crew from channel five."

"I can go snags the brewskis from th' fridge doojigger," Jeff said. Reef looked conflicted after hearing that suggestion. Behind him, Jacob trembled, his brow covered in perspiration. He cracked his knuckles, his demeanor revealing the stark fear that quivered through his chalk-white body. He pressed against a wall, centered inside the Bull's-Eye Ammunition ad.

From the open nose cone emerged a red-clothed woman Legion didn't recognize. Jeff shot her in the head before she took cover. She fell back and hunched over the transport's side, splashing the floor with gray and crimson. Four others emerged, one being the two-headed Schizophrenic who so often accompanied the criminal mastermind Grestlix. Only the sneer on his left face and the sleepy look on his right one overshadowed his tanklike build.

The next invader stepped around his fallen ally, scrambled to one side of the Lasergem, and began flinging rocks at Legion using a Y-shaped stick. A stick? Seriously? Paper airplanes made better ammunition.

"Let's do this afore the ultimate couponing games is come on the broadcast! I loves watchin' people gets kicked up in the head over a half-off ticket!" Jeff tagged a thug with a thin laser beam shot from his fingertip. The thug stumbled back, a rivulet of blood arcing from his bicep.

"It's not the galaxy's official sport for nothing." Aaron chewed his bubblegum noisily, exuding a waft of stale breath.

"I'll acknowledge decorative hairnets before I acknowledge that!" Legion fired. At least couponing had replaced the previous official sport: ultimate slap fighting.

The rock flinger crouched behind the Lasergem's right wing. Legion recognized her: Grestlix, leader of the Houdin clan. Grestlix's voice rang overtop the barrage of pinging light-bullets, the shells bouncing off the ground, and that awful *bang!* Jeff blurted whenever he fired: "Lieutenant Colonel Matross Legion, I have a message from your old friend George Lowensland."

Legion raised an open hand to halt the others. "Everyone, hold your attack. Let the woman speak, but keep ready. Jeff, put away the datasheet. This isn't that kind of message."

"The message is to keep away from us," Grestlix said. "We are the Bad Guys, and we know about your hyperpeople response force. We *will* kill you if you oppose us. You have no chance of winning this war."

"Zat mean we the Good Guys because we fights the Bad Guys?" Jeff said. Legion groaned from the absolute stupidity of such an idea.

Legion stepped to the left to see Grestlix better. She scowled at him.

Her left hand scooped the air in a J-shaped signal. "Bad

Guys, fall back and return to headquarters!"

"Sh-should we follow them?" Aaron cupped his backward-facing baseball cap over his head and eyed Legion's Marsek with trepidation.

"No. Let them go." Legion slid his Marsek into its holster. He didn't want to reignite the battle since his recruits were untrained. His heart plummeted in freefall. Totally untrained.

The surviving Bad Guys filed into the nose cone's darkened access port. The nose cone flipped down when the last enemy had entered, his footsteps pinging against the floor. The Lasergem's thrusters crackled to life in a surge of static discharge, and Legion felt the transport gently push away. The dead woman that slouched over the Lasergem's side slipped onto the floor. The Lasergem withdrew, and scraps of the metal wall slid off with an awful clang.

Wow. No one had died, despite the vastly inexpert group Legion led. His body still shook, his hands still squeezed into death grips, but…everyone had survived. Still, they were sloppy, scattered. No way would his team enter battle without training. They couldn't possibly live through another fight like this.

Jeff tossed away a piece of scrap. "All that for a flippin' message? We gots a recep…a reper…a recrep…some desk guy for that type o' thing." He asked Mark, "Wuzzat a drive-by?"

———

Grestlix barked the order to return to *The Mikazin*

Starship. In the cockpit section of the nearly pitch-black Lasergem, lights shone from the pilot's control panel and reflected off her skin in kaleidoscopic dots. The transport's primary viewscreen, placed across the area where a pressure windshield would stretch in a conventional transport, showed streaked lines of stars to indicate the Lasergem's acceleration.

Grestlix's heart swelled. The team consisted of only six fighters, but they executed their mission excellently, a perfection possible only through her outstanding leadership. She hadn't assessed the "full-blown tastiness" of Intergalactic Protection's apple pies as that hapless halfwit Master Asinine had wanted, but she'd delivered the message: "Stay away. Far away."

Grestlix chuckled. She had acted adeptly today. She marched toward the passenger area of the transport—

A gun emerged from the darkness and its barrel tapped Grestlix's forehead. Huh? A Face Blitzkrieg! Who was this colossal buffoon who threatened her with such menace? "Who dares point this weapon at me? I demand an answer, fool." She chopped the gun barrel away from her forehead.

The shadows rippled. Her adversary emerged. Shock flashed through her body. Adrenaline detonated in her brain.

The adversary was Schizophrenic.

His Face Blitzkrieg met Grestlix's forehead again. "This ain't personal," Lefty said. His lips shifted the toothpick that seemed permanently attached to his tongue.

"You insipid cretin." Grestlix felt as if she fumed steam-whistle smoke from her ears. "You will pay for this insubordination. You hold a gun to my head—our master weapon, no less—and tell me it 'ain't personal'?"

"No." Lefty's speech sounded thick. "It's just business. Well, it's personal, too. You're a toadstool." Lefty regarded Righty. "Shoot her already."

Righty smiled. "Wow. My first assassination." A splash of red exploded over Grestlix's vision.

The last fading words Grestlix heard buzzed from a million universes away. "Someone wake up the pilot before he hits that satellite."

CHAPTER SEVEN
IF THEY'RE NOT HIDING THEIR GOLD,
THEY'RE PLANTING INCRIMINATING
EVIDENCE

"Well, that was easy." Master Asinine crouched over Markiset's fresh corpse. He held a pistol—not a Face Blitzkrieg, but a regular sidearm—from which smoke rose in twisting tendrils. One shot, right to the center of Markiset's forehead. "Cataclysmic" wasn't how Asinine would describe the murder, not like the collision of two planets or the omelet station at the Mikazin clan's Lent buffet last year. But the murder accomplished the job…and its anticlimactic simplicity left him unsatisfied. "A bit *too* easy."

Asinine heard nothing but the white-noise hiss of the filthy overhead vents and the dying outburst of the gunshot. He peered up at Lieutenant IQ 23. Lieutenant IQ 23 shrugged, looking as disappointed with the ease of the assassination as Master Asinine.

Asinine occupied a small, muggy shipping bay with Lieutenant IQ 23 and Braindead standing behind him. In here, he breathed more dust than air. It had been tough to goad Markiset into entering the shipping bay. She was mistrusting.

But after leading her here, Asinine had found her assassination far too effortless.

"She could have put up *some* struggle." Asinine stood and wrinkled his face in dissatisfaction. Huh. He tapped his pistol against a hip, an empty feeling in his heart.

"For what it's worth, sir," Lieutenant IQ 23 said, "you did a fine job."

A short hall stretched out to the left along one wall of the bay and ended at an l-door that now faded with the sound of a mooing cow, his favorite sound setting. The lights outside cast silhouettes of Wiltroh, Requiston, Sikth'nkphth, and Convenient Victim. Sikth'nkphth's slithery tongue flickered so quickly it could put hummingbird wings in second place. The hiss from his pursed lips made him sound as if he'd sprung a leak. If the moron talked sometimes, Asinine would consider him more than some perpetually antisocial nitwit. As things stood, this guy was a jerk.

Wiltroh rumbled into the room with the grace of a thousand-pound bowling ball careening down a staircase. His gray skin rippled with each footstep, which caused Asinine to forcibly suppress a gag.

The four coleaders followed the hall until they reached the bay area. Wiltroh groaned upon spotting Markiset's corpse, and his stomach groaned with him. He probably hadn't eaten in all of thirty seconds. He put a hand to his forehead to block his eyes from the ghastly sight. "Not her, too. This is highly illogical." No, what was illogical was the humongous body mass he was packing.

"Hi, guys." Master Asinine smiled and his hand sprang into a hearty wave. "Great to see you."

"Oh, drop the act," Requiston said in his gratingly high timbre.

Wiltroh crossed his arms. Asinine feared that his life was about to end in one mammoth gulp, provided Wiltroh could find a mouth among all those chins. "We just overheard a message from the mission team."

"Which mission team?"

"The severely undersized one you arranged. Schizophrenic has apparently just assassinated Grestlix. With a Face Blitzkrieg. At your command. And then he called you fashion's biggest bottleneck."

Asinine wore his best look of ham-acted shock. "What? He should have assassinated Grestlix discree-ee-ee—I mean he shouldn't have assassinated Grestlix at all, and by no means did I order him to do it or undersize the team on purpose to ensure her death. Nice save. I mean, I should use my inside voice to say, 'Nice save.'" *Nice save.* "Done."

Wiltroh growled and sharpened his brow. Was he preparing to eat a tree? "What are you talking about?"

"Nothing. But check the basement behind the bomb-and-missile-equipped booby trap. Everybody at the same time. There might be evidence of treachery there."

"We just heard Lefty's confirmation," Requiston said. "He left a message on your viewscreen. We were standing there, listening to him leave it. We heard everything."

"But he lied," Master Asinine said. "You can't prove anything."

"What's left to prove? You almost openly confessed before stammering. You're right now standing over Markiset's dead body, holding a smoking gun!"

Master Asinine looked down at the gun in his hand, plumes of smoke still trickling from its barrel. "Crocking caca!" He threw the gun aside as if its handle had burst into flame. "How did that get in my hand? Lieutenant, did you notice anything?"

Lieutenant IQ 23's face erupted with the same dramatic look Master Asinine wore. "Now that I think about it, sir, I was *wondering* what those devilish leprechauns were up to. They were evidently here to kill Markiset and set you up. They must have planted the gun in your hand while you were being innocent of murdering Markiset."

"There you have it." Master Asinine smiled at the others. "Case closed. Call the coroner."

Wiltroh grabbed his Face Blitzkrieg from behind his back. It looked impish in his hand but wasn't exactly set on tickle like so much of Asinine's armament. That obese pig must have hid an entire arsenal inside his folds of flesh. Sikth'nkphth and Requiston followed suit and unsheathed their Face Blitzkriegs. Convenient Victim was too frightened to pull a weapon out, which led Master Asinine to believe his name wasn't a coincidental translation after all.

"Hey, careful with the Face Blitzkriegs in *The Mikazin Starship*. We could blow out a wall. Or my head." Asinine scrutinized Wiltroh's Face Blitzkrieg and its approaching, blubber-mouthed owner. He crossed his eyes when the weapon's barrel met his nose with a spine-tickling tap.

"None of us ever wanted to follow your juvenile plan," Wiltroh said. "To conquer Renovodomus only because you were laughed out of IP? What rubbish. We wish to conquer it for the simple act of supremacy."

Asinine tapped a finger on his chin. "Huh. That's a much better reason than mine. Can I tack that onto my list?"

"Silence! We only united with you to continue after your inevitable failure." Wiltroh twisted the position of the Face Blitzkrieg underneath Asinine's nose, scraping a nostril with its barrel. Asinine wished he had to sneeze. He also wished he knew how Wiltroh had managed to haul his planet-sized body across the room. "For your treachery, the only logical outcome is to fire this weapon straight at your brain."

"I wouldn't," Asinine said. "I still haven't taught you the secret handshake. It's just like the regular one except secreter."

"Oh, shut *up!*" Wiltroh stomped back a step to his cohorts. "Let us just slay him and his two underlings and then deal with Schizophrenic. At least we won't have to face this dreadful costume any longer." He gestured at Asinine's hip duds.

Requiston screeched agreement and Sikth'nkphth nodded. Wiltroh set his shot at Asinine's head—

—and his temple erupted in a red splash! Asinine looked past his falling body to Sikth'nkphth and Requiston. Requiston spun at the attacker, raised his Face Blitzkrieg, and *his* head blew back in so much detritus that it was difficult to see if the majority of it remained attached. Next Sikth'nkphth fell, an open hole where his temple had been, which was spectacular because Asinine wouldn't have to try pronouncing his name anymore.

Braindead stepped forward, having shot the three light-bullets that left Master Asinine's coconspirators' heads looking like Wiffle balls. He placed the gun barrel against Convenient Victim's temple as if daring him—no, *triple-dog* daring him—to make any abrupt moves. Convenient Victim read the message loud and clear. He only whimpered. Was this really the same guy who painted the town napalm red because a girl refused to go to the prom with him?

"Good job, Braindead." Master Asinine slapped a hand over the Virillian's back. "That's why you're on our side: your crack shot and your ability to brew a fine drink. Mostly your crack shot, though. You can't mix a Blarney Stone cocktail to save your life." He stepped over Wiltroh's corpse but reconsidered and stepped back onto its head. And ground his heel into its eye socket. Twice. Fun.

He grabbed Convenient Victim's chin and dug his fingertips into the flesh. Blood seeped out where his fingernails stabbed. He forced Convenient Victim's chin up so the Trioxidillian faced him. With a glint of evil in his eyes, he gritted his teeth so fiercely he'd be surprised if this wimp's pants remained dry.

Convenient Victim reached for the Face Blitzkrieg in his holster, but Asinine grabbed it from his gentle grip. "I'll take that." He handed the weapon to Braindead.

"Now, you listen to me. You're lucky to be alive, but let's get one thing clear. This coalition was a hoax. Now that I've stolen your manpower, weapons, technology, and soda machines, I have no use for you. I lead and no one disputes that. If you do anything—*anything*—that makes me want to kill you, I will kill you. Understand?"

"Y-yes." Convenient Victim nodded frantically with a profound quiver that told Master Asinine he understood. His tail curled into the ball of hands that he clasped to his chest. This was really the guy who forced enemies to eat all the expired food from his fridge doojigger? He'd had guacamole in there!

"Good. It's time to start my strategy for domination now that I have complete control of the Bad Guys and that you suck. Let's visit my science goons, bring them some cupcakes, and find out how they're doing with loading the Face Blitzkrieg technology into the megalaser.

"But first, Lieutenant, I'm so hungry I could eat a horse as big as a pony. Let's go blitzkrieg my face in an altogether different way. I want to celebrate my rash enthusiasm with an upturned helmet full of Froot Loops. And not the old-person kind with bitter melon and prunes, but the real deal. I can't conquer Renovodomus without my nine essential nutrients."

Lieutenant IQ 23 held up a glinting spoon. "It's part of your complete breakfast, sir."

CHAPTER EIGHT
LATRINE HUMOR

The smacking and grunting of combat popped around Legion like angry fireworks. Though not real combat—only a training scenario in Intergalactic Protection's simulator gym—it felt as real as the real thing, especially with Jeff urinating into the simulation fire drums that kept the simulation hobos warm. "Jeff, stop peeing on military property!" To what had life come when Legion had to bark that command with a straight face? "How much urine can you even hold?"

"Normal," Jeff tossed over his shoulder. "Normal plus one."

"Your bladder is the stuff of legends. You're exactly like our lunch lady."

"Jeff"—Mark ducked a simulation combatant's left hook—"have you been drinking liquid coolants again? It's not blueberry Kool-Aid. We've gone over this, Jeff!"

"Except for the taste an' smell an' way I throws up whenever I drinked it, it ain't *not* blueberry Kool-It!"

"That's precisely the opposite of what I just said."

The team's training gym remained unfurnished, but Intergalactic Protection lent this one to Legion, which he snatched up for an hour. The l-tech it used to conjure up the training scenarios set Legion's nerves on fire, but he kept his distance from wherever it popped up. After years of practice, he was good at that.

From the observation deck overlooking the gym one floor above, Aaron Khouri orchestrated the seething war simulation that at one point included aliens from *Space Invaders* and, for some reason, the bearded dwarf from *Golden Axe*. He was still a step up from their previous computer techie: one of those windup monkeys that crashed cymbals together when you turned its crank. Reef sat with him, following orders from on high that he stay out of training to prevent overuse of his hyperability, this confidential hyperability Legion knew nothing about. Reef's profile said, "Hyperability: information classified. Please make our sponsor, Random Impositions, happy by including that bearded dwarf fro—" Oh. So *that* was why.

The haunt control's ability to summon and dissolve l-objects presented a simulation battlefield scenario: simulation insurgents staged a simulation coup, now threatening to simulation-execute a simulation high-ranking politician if their simulation demands were refused. The haunt control even infected the air with the piquant sting of simulation burned oil. The insurgents were robots dressed as simulation Virillian guerrillas, the linoleum floor was the simulation lawn that sprawled away from the politician's simulation estate, and the gym's west side was Jeff's simulation latrine. Too bad Jeff was peeing an endless stream of nonsimulation urine.

Everett shot to flight on thick wings, launched himself at an insurgent, threw a talon-crammed punch. The insurgent retaliated with a jab thudding against Everett's cheek. Everett spun backward at the false grass, and his head conked against a fabricated tree trunk. Out cold, but an insurgent was already zeroing in on the opportunity to finish him off. Legion fired a light-bullet at the insurgent, and its head evaporated. "Mark, protect Everett. Jacob, you're backup."

Mark nodded curtly and dealt a decisive knee to an insurgent's robotic groin. Jacob, taking cover behind a wrought-iron fence, poked his head above the barbed tips and clutched his pistol against his chest. He shuddered. Nope. Not engaging in battle this time, Legion determined. Or the next ten or eleven times. Why would a kid so enthusiastic about *Halo* cower during a training simulation?

"Ghiglix, you have two insurgents on your six. Mark, behind you. Jeff, stop trying to count to six. Jacob, shoot blindly into the air. Jeff, seriously stop trying to count to six."

"R-roger." Jacob ended up blasting a simulation bird into a cloud of feathers. A squawk marked the bird's demise.

A blur zipped past Legion and skated up a twenty-foot-high catwalk in the time Legion took to blink. Ghiglix.

Mark had finished with an insurgent—toasted its insides—and tossed it aside where it clattered to the grass. It fizzled out white foam from its damaged fissures and circuits. Jeff redirected his stream onto it, chirping something about writing his name in the snow. Terrans.

"Legion!" Mark's voice cut through the frenzy of combat. "On your ten."

Legion glanced left—"Jeff, what did I tell you about counting to every number someone shouts? That's a double digit you're playing with"—as, above him, a wreckage of wires and spiral-cut gears snarled aflame. He shielded his head and, when the maelstrom of machinery stopped, unblocked his face to see Mark cut a nod at him. Legion saluted a thank you.

By now, Jacob had conjured two duplicates of himself and shot them into combat. His hyperability in action. Those duplicates charged through the battle with fists and legs careening into insurgents. After only moments, they sidled up beside Jeff and helped him soak the false lawn with urine. Jeff high-fived them. Legion wanted to slap the back of his head. *Hands on deck when you're spraying, soldier!*

What was Jeff even thinking?

———

—ngleheimer Schmit, that's is my name, too. Jeff swung his stream into the simulation gutter where it produced a sizzling froth. *Whenever we goes out, the people always shouts—*

———

Legion decided Jeff was no longer allowed on the furniture.

He ducked an insurgent's determined swing, felt the wind whistle above him, thrust his Marsek into the insurgent's mouth, pulled the trigger. Gears and mechanical brain matter detonated out its skull. A splash of cold lubricant speckled Legion's cheek. He wiped the lubricant onto a sleeve.

Without turning, Jeff pointed a fist backward and splashed a ray of light at an insurgent. The insurgent's midsection sprayed sparks and gears across the lawn. "Kerpunch!" Jeff yelled and went back to marking his territory.

"Holy horsewhip, so many insurgents!" Jacob toppled out from behind the fence's chipped staves as if something had regurgitated him. His eyes were as wide as floodlights, his Adam's apple bobbling. He sputtered off a quick shot at an insurgent and scattered its throat. The slight recoil swung his aim off course. He blasted a chunk out of a ballast, which crumpled and collapsed onto a deactivated civ-tran. Mark rolled out of the way to avoid being crushed. C minus for effort, D plus for playing well with others.

An uproar from Legion's right. Ghiglix's sharp war cry overpowered the clank of battle. Legion glanced over, spotted an insurgent wrestling with Ghiglix on the catwalk that led from a simulation parking garage to the ground level. His teeth visible in a grimace, Ghiglix clasped fingers with the insurgent in a dangerous game of mercy. Reality—

—rippled?

Legion reached out—and felt only thickened air. In his antennae—sound. It fizzed down to a muffled version of existence. A sensation like a lightning bolt climaxed in his brain. He blinked. It took effort. Shutting his eyelids felt like shutting them around cotton balls. He clenched his fists carefully so as not to squeeze off a shot from his Marsek since his toes were dear to him. The lawn—fake? real? did it matter?—was marred with brush fires. It liquefied into an Intergalactic Protection hangar bay, the catwalk into an embarking ramp leading to a Fireball starship, Ghiglix into— *what the*—into Sopher? The training scenario dispersed, and Legion found himself elsewhere. Found himself back in Intergalactic Protection's hangar bay. Wait, was this where he should be? Yeah…probably. Why not? Yes. Yes! Definitely. Existence had righted itself. He checked the insurgent who fought Sopher—

He growled. A burgundy filter suddenly veiled everything.

The insurgent was Lowensland. That vile reprobate. Legion's forehead ached with conflict. He gripped his Marsek. His legs, his core, his chest, his arms locked themselves in succession. The salvo of enraged battle became a warning claxon that melded into one ululation. It broke only to alert him of Blazing Gasoline's upcoming fire sale. Literal term.

Legion couldn't speak. He only bellowed, trudging through reality in slow motion. He fired once, twice at Lowensland, whose arm exploded and fell in an oily shower of blood too black to be a Terran's. Legion pecked off another salvo. Three light-bullets carved lines through the air. Burst Lowensland's head like a water balloon. Hatched his shoulder. Slit Sopher's scalp. Sopher screamed—in a voice that wasn't his?

Lowensland fell. He became an insurgent. Sopher melted away into Ghiglix. The hangar bay became the lawn. The starship in the hangar's corner became Jeff, whose bladder could evidently put out a forest fire. Almost impressive.

Had the hangar bay been an apparition? Was this reality? Was Blazing Gasoline really holding a fire sale? If Legion's surroundings changed again, could he put in a request?

The insurgent flopped across the catwalk. Ghiglix collapsed on top of him. From the sky—now the gym's characterless ceiling—buzzed a cutoff signal as the haunt control ended the masquerade of the training scenario. Legion couldn't feel his Marsek in his hand. Maybe he'd dropped it. Around him, the haunt control repainted the distant horizon as the gym's steel walls. The scaly Virillian skin of the insurgents frothed into the titanium chassis of the robots, which powered down with an eerie whir. The parking garage revealed itself as the gym's observation deck. In the deck's vista window, Aaron's ample eyes stared down at Legion. Reef was already sprinting to the stairwell leading down to the gym. Jeff uttered a word as if waking from a dream, and the last drops of his titanlike flood diverted onto Everett's shoe. "Where them hobos gone? I was winnin' a contest. Try an' guess what it was."

"Game over, advertising victims," the haunt control said. "Warning: training combatant injured. Warning: only two days remain for low rates on diuretic insurance at the law firm of Hammond, Another Hammond, and Yet a Third Hammond. Warning: the insanity doesn't stop when it comes to garroting cable at Murder Depot. Get your length of piano wire today!"

The catwalk on which Ghiglix lay shifted, grunted, and sank to the ground. At least it drowned out the electronic saleswoman's pitch for civ-trans, now available with brake pads.

"Warning: Murder Depot's sale is now over due to our shift manager's new manslaughter charges. Wish him well with our new courtroom vuvuzelas."

Legion now felt his Marsek in his hand, threw it aside, apologized to Jacob for the Marsek-shaped bruise the recruit would soon suffer, and fell into a slide at Ghiglix's side. "Ghiglix, talk to me." He shook Ghiglix, but the Fleeson remained facedown on the linoleum. "Ghiglix—wake—up!" Legion swatted aside his cross necklace and shook the Fleeson harder.

Reef and Jacob hurried over. Jacob checked Ghiglix's breathing and measured his pulse. "Seems normal." He inspected the gash that crosshatched the fold of his brow, a shallow line oozing blood. "We have to get him to the infirmary. Trust me. I used to work for my dad as a transport attendant. 'Ten days without an accident' was a banner event at the Refensil Recharge Station. News crews showed up."

Reef traced a finger along the blood that drew a line

down Ghiglix's brow. "I'll call a medbot."

Legion staggered back, only a bystander witnessing this scene from the sideline. He tingled, felt his senses become feathery. The report of the gunshot that ruined Sopher's life thrashed around his mind. And when the report finally petered out, Patton's voice replaced it with a spectral reminder: "Control your resentment or it will jeopardize everyone. Taste this gratuity trail mix. It's like an exploded granola bar but without the gunpowder residue this time."

Reef examined Ghiglix's brow more closely. "Medbot's on its way with pizza. Ghiglix gets a free IV bag if no one delivers in half an hour." He shrugged at Jacob. "Seemed like a good deal."

"So IP wants media names?" Jacob cleared his throat. "You think they'd go for Jacob, You Stay on Base and Eat This Delicious Sandwich?"

———

"Lieutenant Colonel!"

Legion jerked at the sound of his name.

Forty-five minutes had passed since the medbot had rushed Ghiglix to the sick bay. A barking directive had summoned Legion to Patton's office. Might as well have dragged him in by the ear. Now he sat, never before feeling so boiling hot in his own skin, sitting on this chair that had never felt so rigid, agonizing under this rebuke from a Patton who had never scolded anyone so severely.

Patton didn't even twiddle his moustache while he

screamed, red-faced, continuing the half-hour tirade on Legion's irresponsibility and refusal to at least *try* Snack Cesspool's new line of designer cookies. Legion couldn't say he didn't deserve the reproach. He studied the carpet as intently as if he were memorizing it, struggling not to detect that hint of oatmeal on Patton's breath. Those cookies could contain all the fiber that science dared to pack in, but they still smelled stale.

In one hand, Patton clutched a deactivated datasheet: Legion's therapy attendance report. The real report, not the forged one. "You"—Patton paused to loom over his desk at Legion and gulp down another cookie—"endangered the lives of"—he licked the oatmeal debris off his fingers—"everyone in that training session!"—and dusted the crumbs from his moustache. "You sure you don't want a bite? You can't even taste the barbiturates."

Legion could only flicker his eyes up at Patton before returning to the carpet's brown fibers. "Sir." He fingered his collar to release the heat sweltering under his uniform. Didn't help. "I should remind you that this isn't the time for us to share a snack and that barbiturates affect the central nervous system and cause mental afflictions such as bipolar disease."

Patton's rage clicked on again. "Bipolar is a disorder, not a—" He paused. "Let's not get off track here, Lieutenant Colonel. You were given a specific recovery regimen, and a deeper investigation into your attendance reveals that you showed up to not *one single session.*" He flung the datasheet at

Legion and pounded a fist on his desk. The computer inside the desktop ordered a cinnamon cappuccino and muttered an ouch.

Legion's stomach felt like a flash grenade had detonated inside it.

"Your appraisal revealed that you forged your therapy records." Patton's breathing calmed.

"Therapy? How could IP ask me to just…" Legion tried to put a name to every emotion surfing the tsunami in his head.

"Lieutenant Colonel, how could you lie to us? To *me*? Why didn't you attend therapy? We could have helped you forget about all that—"

"Helped me forget? That's precisely why I didn't attend! I didn't want to just *forget* Sopher's sacrifice!" Legion discovered he was clutching his pant legs.

Patton waited a beat. It lasted six seconds, Legion determined from the clock that hung on the wall. "This isn't about—" Patton breathed deeply through his nose. He flicked something out of his eye. "You lied to me. You were like a son."

"I know. You bought me a bicycle for my birthday once. It was weird." Legion bounced his eyes to the window that displayed a surly overcast sky outside. "It also wasn't my birthday."

"Look at me when we're reliving awkward moments, Lieutenant Colonel."

Legion did. Tried anyway, but again he deflected his gaze after only a second when he detected the hurt and dismay in Patton's eyes. Patton's face was as red as a sunburn. He'd probably tried the new gratuity tanning beds.

Patton stepped back, the honors on his uniform's breast jingle-belling. "Ghiglix is recovering. The docs slathered healing putty on him. Stuff smells like vinegar. Tastes like rubber." Patton waved the comment off. "Don't judge me. I was eating onion rings at the time." He rubbed the back of his neck and faced the window's miserable display. "Lieutenant Colonel, you assured Intergalactic Protection you were fit for combat. So did the psych assessments you forged. We placed people under your command. Intergalactic Protection brass… They want me to…They…" Another pause. Another sigh. Another cookie. Patton's voice cracked when he said, "I'm ordered to strip you of your rank. Field Marshal Hullinger wants you gone. I fought him, but in the end, I couldn't help matters. You're lucky he's not arresting you for endangering your subordinates. I'm sorry, Lieutenant Colonel." Patton's esteemed posture weakened. "It's been an honor."

Legion barely registered sensation. He felt as if he were tilting forward into a void. "This is real?" He bolted to his feet. Whoa. A head rush forced him to brace a hand on Patton's desk. That cappuccino order became a double. "I'm out?"

"I'm afraid so, son. Pack up. Leave your sidearm and gratuities on your bedside table. I'll look the other way if you want to keep the tortellini truffles."

"I don't eat—" Legion stopped himself. "Yes, sir."

CHAPTER NINE
SO MANY SECRET WEAPONS, SO FEW SHOWDOWNS

Master Asinine squiggled his butt deeper into his cherished throne. Couldn't quite get comfortable. Maybe because the throne was a stack of milk crates. But since Lieutenant IQ 23 stopped visiting when he sat on the *throne* throne—you know the one—this would have to do. And this one had armrests.

The room was musky with dust. Asinine smelled nothing but the chalky residue that seeped under his clothes and dirtied his skin, undoing his hydrogen sulfide shower. From overhead speakers, his musical choice—the latest whining from the boy band Your Parents Must Hate Us by Now—fluttered down like confetti. The band opened their hearts on subjects such as lonely girls that were so fine, cheaters and players, and geography tests, in order of socioeconomic relevance.

The l-door to this room—his bowtie closet—faded with a harpsichord's lilt. Lieutenant IQ 23 entered with Braindead, the universe's most devoted bosom buddy, on his heels. The underlit tone lent a covert slant to their arrival, though this visit was probably for nothing more than to read Asinine his bedtime story: the options on Octopus Buffet's brunch menu. There was a surprise twist to the number five special.

"Sir, I come bearing news you'll want to hear immediately." Lieutenant IQ 23 scratched his cheek and took position by the throne's right armrest. He dropped the menu.

Asinine scooched deeper into his throne's seat warmer: a hotplate on the toaster setting. "I already heard about the rooster trained to smoke two packs a day. I'm up on Faux News's top animal-related and addiction-related stories. Did you know there's a platypus that drinks more cups of coffee before nine than most people drink all day? It's decaf, but still. Inspiring."

"You know I find all forms of overachievement in the animal kingdom fascinating, sir, but I come with more pertinent news."

Master Asinine lifted one butt cheek and grabbed the hash brown crisping underneath. "What news is more percolate than an animal's chemical dependencies?" He spoke through a full mouth.

"Intergalactic Protection relieved Matross Legion of duty."

"Someone took a dump on his behalf?"

"Very close, sir. I mean they discharged him."

"Say what, say what?" Asinine sprang out of his throne, and the stack of crates serving as his backrest collapsed with a clatter of plastic knocks. Crock. Building the orthopedic curves had taken, like, half an hour and stuff.

"Discharged, Lieutenant? You mean they fired him? Why would they fire him? Only eight years ago they upgraded his position to Supreme Beekeeper!"

"That was two days ago, sir, and that rank was never confirmed." Lieutenant IQ 23 lowered his voice to a portentous whisper. "Sir, this puts at risk your plan to face him in history's biggest game of hide-and-seek."

"No fair!" Asinine clobbered an armrest. His second hash brown dropped off the seat of his pants despite the ketchup sticking it there. "Fine. Intergalactic Protection has forced my hand. How is my chief science thug coming along with the Face Blitzkrieg superlaser?"

"Old Mrs. Whatley has the technology loaded and waiting, sir."

"Excellent. Reward her with a set of gold-studded knitting needles. No longer will we attack in two days. Today, we force IP to rehire Legion. We call him and his agents out. Thus begins the first sixty-eighth of my master plan." He clutched the air. "I won't be Intergalactic Protection's kicking monkey for long. I'll *rule* this galaxy. Lieutenant, find me the closest location with enough hiding spaces and free parking, for we attack right after my footbath.

"And prepare my secret weapon."

"The hose that squirts milk out of your nose at the slightest hint of a good knock-knock joke?"

"The other secret weapon." Asinine snapped his fingers.

"But thanks for reminding me of the Milk Splooger Nine Thousand. Sploogie will come in handy at my next colonoscopy."

CHAPTER TEN
AS SEEN ON TV

"Colonel Patton has arrived," the haunt control in Legion's former office said.

Standing at his desk—well, not *his* desk anymore—Legion jumped with surprise at the haunt control's report. The plastiglass juice bottle in his grip spurted orange liquid when he crushed it reflexively. Sticky juice showered the desk and his hands. He leaned forward and clicked his tongue at the mess. Great. Just great. He flicked droplets from his fingers, splashing it on his military college graduate's degree and the keepsakes he'd stuffed into a box he was using to empty the office. He tossed the remains of his drink into the trash ionizer next to the desk. The desk activated a self-cleaning mechanism that burned the mess of juice off its top and scorched his apple. Now the rank odor of burned fruit flooded the office. Within seconds, the desk was clean, though the desktop unit had executed a few unwanted commands from its touch screen. That explained why his walls were purple and oinking at him now.

Legion hadn't even finished emptying his office after his discharge, and Patton now visited him? Why the interruption?

Maybe Patton was delivering his severance package of gratuity haircut vouchers. Yes, haircut vouchers for a member of a hairless race.

A knock at his door. "Colonel Patton has arrived." Yeah, yeah. The haunt control sounded more desperate than it ever had before, though Legion knew these announcements were identical.

Another knock. A voice followed the knock. "Patton here." Patton there.

Legion sighed at the stickiness on his hands. "Control, acknowledge. Unlock door." Wait! No sooner had Legion finished his sentence did he realize IP had already converted his door from a sliding one to l-tech. He ducked for cover behind the desk—but the door vaporized without incident. Close call, though.

Patton rushed in, his steps uncharacteristically heavy and his expression unusually worried. "Lieutenant Colonel Legion, something has come up."

Legion dropped a datasheet into his box. "I thought I wasn't Lieutenant Colonel Legion anymore, sir. You discharged me a few hours ago."

Patton spoke his next words as if going over a speed bump. "We need you back."

"Yeah. Right. I've had ex-girlfriends take longer to regret breakups." Legion put another keepsake into the box, waiting for someone to pull the trigger on the punchline to this joke. He trusted Patton with his life, but he didn't trust IP that this "we need you back" shenanigan was real. Whatever IP had convinced Patton of was a lie. Maybe his belief was a result of Mind Playmate's new truth cough serum.

Patton rushed to Legion's desk. His hand brushed his moustache and mussed its pointed end. "Recent news changed your status. Open a viewscreen, Lieutenant Colonel."

Legion paused from placing another datasheet in the box. "Forgive my incredulity, sir, but what is Intergalactic Protection's game? Hullinger discharged me for as long as he takes to run to the doughnut shop."

"Don't be silly. Ant Farm Desserts delivers now." Patton pulled a raisin doughnut out of a pocket, unwrapped it, and made Legion wonder if those were really raisins scurrying around it. "Anyway, a situation has arisen—and you're the only one who can bail us out."

Legion had to speak above the office's animal noises, which had progressed from oinking to clucking. "I can't open a viewscreen. I'm officially discharged."

"The haunt control will accept your command, Lieutenant Colonel. Field Marshal Hullinger was quick to relist you in its database."

Legion didn't know what to believe anymore. He tested his luck. "Open viewscreen, use preset dimensions." None of this widescreen format Jeff had been toying with.

A familiar click sounded and, to Legion's surprise, a viewscreen grew from nothing into a five-foot square against the opposite wall. Soon an image appeared on its surface, a

Letchtech logo that pulsated as the viewscreen awaited its next command.

"What's this about, sir? What am I supposed to command the viewscreen to display?"

"Check the news on channel fourteen, Lieutenant Colonel." Patton placed a hand on Legion's shoulder, but that hand quickly removed itself and went to his moustache. "Lowensland's plan is ahead of our expectations. Our new task force will have to fight before they start their training."

Legion's mouth hung open as if on loose hinges. "What? That's impossible. We had four days. It's only been two! Those soldiers haven't been trained enough to enter battle before training." And the survival of Renovodomus depended on the one soldier who produced moronic sentences such as that.

Legion gathered himself. "Sir, they're not ready. We're sorely outnumbered." The clucking became mooing.

"They have to. Private Ghiglix is already recovering, and your team has been apprised of the situation. Lieutenant Colonel, am I catching you during some sort of farm fantasy?" Patton had been twirling his moustache, but he stopped. He fidgeted and reached for it again. "Never mind. Things have gone from bad to worse. Lowensland accelerated his timeline. He's taken hostages and claims to have a super destructive secret weapon. He says he'll use that weapon if you're not reinstated and sent to him for playtime, as he put it. We're not sure if this secret weapon is his milk hose, but if it isn't...

Lieutenant Colonel, this could mean the end of Renovodomus.

"Lowensland was one of our own who stole our secrets and escaped, so the public will view this as an act of radicalism that Intergalactic Protection indirectly caused. We stand to lose a *lot* of capital on this. So Field Marshal Hullinger himself is willing to reinstate you on the condition that you agree to attend therapy. For *real* this time. He'll sign the datawork himself." Patton tapped Legion's desktop with a single finger. "He doesn't want to lose these fresh-from-the-ant-farm doughnuts."

Legion's hands trembled and his breath came in uneven gasps. Without training? Only some of his charges were even minimally ready for battle!

His veins iced upon hearing the despondency in his superior's tone, the unheard sigh that punctuated each word. If something unsettled Patton, it was best to act fast. "Viewscreen, acknowledge"—he swallowed down a bubble of anxiety—"activate broadcast, transmission channel fourteen. The *real* channel fourteen, not that public access junk."

The Letchtech logo shrank into the upper-left corner of the viewscreen's display to make room for the channel fourteen broadcast. A commanding voice boomed even before the image appeared, that same voice that caused Legion's soggy legs to harden to steel. The odor of burned apples strengthened in his mind.

"—thank you, Lieutenant, for that descriptive weather report: still sunny enough for Legion to come out and die."

Lowensland's accursed voice. Legion's anxiety became rage, given voice in a growl through canine-clenched teeth. His organs churned in his belly.

On the viewscreen, Lowensland's mouth cast a toothy smile at the camera facing him. His backdrop was a concrete room barren of features except for its dungeonlike and paint-weary walls. And what was with that costume he wore?

"Lieutenant, let's get a running total on how much viewers have donated."

An offscreen voice whispered, "Sir, this isn't a telethon. It's a call-out."

"Whoops. Forgot." Lowensland faced the camera and curled his fingers in a grasp. "But don't let that stop you from donating. Anyway, to bring the viewers up to speed, 'Operation: Operation' is going excellently according to our master plan. So excellently is it going according to our master plan that we've actually figured out that it is, indeed, our master plan. There was some confusion there, but it's been cleared up, thanks in no small part to coffee.

"And that has brought us here, to this recharge station we've expropriated—my mom said I could if I cleaned my starship—to force Intergalactic Protection to reinstate Legion to his former position.

"And, now, Legion, my friend." Lowensland's fist whipped at the camera and, by extension, at Legion. "Your time has come. You and your new team shall come to the United Recharge Station on Tenth Street and One-Tenth of a

Tenth Street, on Gaia. It is time to finish this." A whisper aimed through the corner of his mouth found its way off camera. "Psst. Braindead, pan over to the theater."

The camera view shifted to the right and found a Gharalgian tied to a picnic table. The Gharalgian wore a full-body mechanic's impact suit stained with oil. Above the picnic table, a sign swayed under a fan and a light panel. The sign proclaimed, in blue crayon, "Theater of Agony." The Gharalgian, writhing but failing to break the laser rope that bound his limbs, grunted through a grease-spotted cloth.

"Hello again, Legion and other fans of mine." Lowensland slid into the camera's view, his grin big enough to swallow his fist. "Legion, if you refuse to accept my challenge, here's a little demonstration of what's in store." He displayed what looked like a modified pistol to the screen, turning it over so his audience could see both sides. "This is my Face Blitzkrieg. Witness how unfriendly it can be to someone's face. Heh. This'll make you shoot brain kazoos out your eyeholes."

"What has that fiend concocted now?" Legion stamped closer to the viewscreen. His hand found its way to his mouth and cupped it. He felt numb, a void sensation he hadn't felt since zero-gravity training.

Lowensland pulled the trigger. From the barrel ripped not a light-bullet but—and Legion had to blink to believe the sight—an undulating ring of bright light that bolted toward the bound Gharalgian.

The Gharalgian had only the time to scream louder

through the gag, his eyes bright, red, and unblinking. The ring, like a warping of reality, cut through his face and midsection, deforming and twisting the organs, spurting blood and orange acids. The Gharalgian's face bent inward, crushed at the nose and molded to the insides of his cheeks. Smeared jawbones and cartilage cracked out the sides of his head and sliced open the back of his neck. It seemed as if Alaphus had finger-painted reality, spreading the man's facial features together. The skin on his face, now meatloaf and hanging from strands of tissue, broke free and slid to the ground with a slurp that made Legion's stomach twist.

Legion slammed his hands over the viewscreen, wanting to leap through and tear that monster in half.

"Lieutenant, grab his wallet," Lowensland said to someone off camera. He rushed to the picnic table that now held his victim in a visage of horror that would last forever. Closed casket. He brandished a pointer, which he used to pick at the man's smeared features. "As you can see, my new favorite toy has blitzkrieged our friend's face here"—using the pointer, he tapped the man's skinless cheek—"here"—the man's skewed mouth—"here"—the man's wonky neck—"and here"—the ear. He winked at the camera, stepping aside so his lieutenant could scuttle past to search the dead man's pockets.

"And that, Legion, is just a small demonstration of what I have the power to do if you don't show up in the next hour." Lowensland checked his wrist as if searching for something inside his bunching sleeve. "Or so. I have no watch, so…" He shrugged. "Lieutenant, see if he has a watch."

"He doesn't, sir, but this coffee cup rim in his wallet says he won a free muffin."

Once again, Lowensland returned to his audience. "And what if you don't show up at all?" He tilted his head down though his eyes remained glued to his audience. Evil whimsy played across his shadowed features. "We've developed a Face Blitzkrieg superlaser, one with a caliber powerful enough to bathe the entire planet of Gaia in blitzkrieg madness."

Patton's hand detached from his moustache, which had been twisted to a spiral. "That madman plans to soak Gaia's entire population in *that?*"

Legion was already grabbing his Marsek and checking its charge reading. "Not if I'm there to stop him."

"Good luck, Lieutenant Colonel. You'll need it." Patton placed a hand on Legion's back. "Also, Hullinger doesn't want to fire you again. He hates reclaiming gratuities you've already touched."

"So, Legion, I will expect you within the hour. I'll wait right here." Lowensland sat on the picnic table. He surveyed the corpse next to him with a grumble of revulsion and then shoved it away. "And hurry. We still have not discovered the difference between Coke and Pepsi, and *time is running out!*"

Lowensland's face softened. "By the way, hi, girls. I like galactic domination, bootlickers, megalomania, evening walks in the park with ice cream, and rocking your socks off. Call me sometime." He clicked his tongue softly. Both hands pointed to the camera, which he teasingly shot with finger guns. "Because if you don't love ice cream, you must be a terrorist."

As the mooing became neighing, Legion's shoulders slackened, and he now knew much, much more than he ever wished to know.

"Okay, time to tune into the ultimate couponing finals."

"Sir, we're still on the air."

"We are?" Lowensland said, the words sneaking out one side of his mouth. "Lieutenant, quick. Keep the flow going."

The camera pivoted left to present his lieutenant, who glanced around in alarm. Caught unexpectedly in the public's watchful eye, he grew a nervous smile that faltered. "Hi, uh, my name's…uhm…I don't remember…uh…and, well, you see, uhm…uhhmm…" He shuddered, looked left, and then right. His uneasy grin returned. His legs kicked an awkward cancan and he fanned out his arms. A hollow singing voice took him over. "Oh, Danny boy…the pipes, the pipes are calling…" A masked Virillian stumbled across the background, a dinner plate balanced on his upward-turned nose and one spinning on each index finger.

"Seriously." Patton eyed the viewscreen with an expression of revulsion. "Good luck with whatever this fight degrades into. *Whatever* it degrades into."

The singing Terran walked across the screen, juggling bowling pins.

CHAPTER ELEVEN
FLYING IN ANY RANDOM DIRECTION

Twenty minutes had passed since Legion had viewed Lowensland's broadcast. Lowensland hadn't given Legion any coordinates with which to find him—only the planet and some street names—so Legion had to locate the recharge station himself. Finally successful, he and his charges now raced to Lowensland—and their doom—inside a Trojan-class Flagstar transport that Intergalactic Protection had provided.

Legion had rarely seen a Flagstar, but what he had first noted upon entering was its lack of interior space. Its crew area consisted of only one room: a passenger deck merged with its crowded cockpit. Legion's seven fighters sat arrayed in its ten seats. Make that nine: Jeff had pulled one out on a dare from Jacob.

Legion sat in the pilot's chair, forced into a slouch under the slanted ceiling of the hollowed nose cone. The venom that fueled his brain felt red hot. Lowensland would die today. Legion would kill that living mishap himself, just as that living mishap had killed Sopher. He tightened his fists over the buttons on the transport's control panel. Legion could have prevented Sopher's death, could have remembered his sidearm. Forget controlling his resentment. He'd like to control that flickering Check Engine light, though.

He'd ordered his seven agents to stay behind him. If anyone were to die today, it would be him. He wouldn't lose anyone else, not after Sopher.

Footsteps approached from the passenger deck that was crammed into the transport's rear. Jeff shuffled forward, stooped under the slanted roof of the cockpit, and leaned over the damaged navigator's chair beside Legion. "Media names," he said.

"What?" Legion tried to concentrate on the data-stuffed diagnostic monitors that flanked the pressure windshield. Why couldn't IP have found someone with navigation experience to read these monitors? Legion could use a navigator. He performed the task dreadfully.

"Media names," Jeff said. "You says IP wants us to gets media names. An' the coolest hype-people teams haves 'em. We a hype-people team now, too, right? Ya know, like Cosm'naut Chimp's Galactic Monkey Squad. Can we haves media names? *Way awesome* ones? C'mon! They helps us for when we goes all undercover 'n' stuff and they keeps us from gettin' our butts übered open in public—"

"What did I say about using that verb in the same sentence as *butt?*"

"—so we all discussed media names in th' back. I calls my brotha Burnout, 'cause he a pyro an' he gets anxious all th' time 'bout me. Reef's stickin' wit' Reef 'cause he don't wants a media name on account o' not blabbin' about his hyper'bility. Aaron's use Ace Spandex 'cause he says his impact suit rides up kinda like spandex."

Aaron interjected, "Really? That was a joke name! Now I sound like home video's most conceited fitness instructor!"

"Everett's gonna goes wit' Harrier 'cause o' them wings. And he's got bushy eyebrows so it makes way total sense. An' Ghiglix moves so, *so* quick fast"—Jeff spat out his version of the sound of whipping wind—"like that. So he gonna be Mermansion—"

"For the last time, it's Momentum!" Ghiglix threw himself back in his chair. The wound on his head must have throbbed because he clutched at the bandage. "Do I have to home-school you on that word?"

"And I've decided," a silhouetted body that must have been Jacob said, "since I multiply, you can call me Franchise, master of market saturation. Taking over your favorite strip mall or quick-stop shopping center…*soon*!" Jacob cracked his knuckles proudly.

Jeff thumbed himself and puffed his chest. "An' check me out, check me out. I'm gonna be Grandmaster Awesome XTK 'cause I'm gonna kicks th' most crock! Ain't that so cool? Ain't it fierce/"

From the back, Mark said, "Jeff, you know what happens when you make up acronyms. Your brain thinks you're spelling and you get migraines."

Legion brushed Jeff away. "Okay, okay. Jeff—

Grandmaster Awestruck—whatever."

"What should we names you? Colonel, Lieutenant, Big Cheese? Or somethin' else? Pet, Lovey-Dovey, Sweet Cheeks? Or ya likes food names? Lamb Chop, Honey, Cupcake?" Jeff shrugged. "Mustard?"

"Just…just call me Legion. Can we discuss this later? I'm concentrating on reaching Gaia's orbit. And food media names are about as ridiculous an idea as electing a couch as president of Renovodomus."

Reef squeaked out of his chair. "Hey, President Couch gave us the lowest unemployment rate in decades."

"He polarized the constituency!" Sweat covered Legion's forehead and produced, on top of the shimmer, a single bead that trickled down his brow.

"We goes wit' Mustard. It's gonna sounds way fierce. 'You just got a taste o' the fist…o' Mustard.' That can be ya battle cry." Jeff proudly strode back to the crew area of the transport. "I'm a good helper today."

Legion sent a silent prayer and squeezed the cross on his necklace. His finger found the small bump where that bullet had struck. The impending battle would prove fatal to most. He knew that, but he hoped it wasn't true. At this moment more than any other, he and his soldiers needed the protection of Alaphus.

"How 'bout Barbecue Sauce?" Jeff asked.

CHAPTER TWELVE
NOT HELPING

Master Asinine wobbled into the repair bay, misjudging a step before stabilizing. The noxious fumes of the recharge modules were an olio of toxic vapors. He sensed the fumes breaking his coordination. He tried catching himself on a rotted doorframe, but the wood broke off where he grabbed it.

The Bad Guys had shanghaied (Asinine had been into vocabulary improvement lately) a recharge station for their showdown with Legion and his litter of kittens. The repair bay opened to the exterior by way of retractable windows as tall as the front garage itself. Asinine shambled toward those retractable windows but tripped over tools and machinery that littered the repair bay: a wrench here, a drill there. Nothing exciting, though. Not even a chainsaw backscratcher.

The antiquity in this technological fossil of a station overwhelmed him. Gaia was the only planet in Renovodomus that teemed with life. With a population in the billions, the rest of Gaia was lush with gadgetry, electronics, and with-it-ness. Aside from the sparse greenery in boring, underdeveloped countries—and that greenery remained only to balance the chemicals spewed out of the powerful nations—beautiful metal coated Gaia. So it was no wonder no one visited this station, with its manual this and hand-operated that. All this place needed to punch itself up was an automated recharge module or a ballistic missile assembly to annihilate nonpaying customers. Obviously, asking his underlings to seize a fun recharge station was too much. They captured one equipped by cavemen. It made the ferocious sting of the chemicals that clouded Asinine's nostrils even more potent.

Thirty Bad Guy minions mingled in the repair bay where Master Asinine stumbled. They congregated around the six overdriven Warbird transports the Bad Guys had used to arrive at this technology-devoid recharge station. Those Warbirds now filled the repair bay with the chemical odor that hindered Asinine's coordination.

The Bad Guy minions were the generic no-names of the business. Dressed in standout red shirts to improve Asinine's chances of survival, the generics had forced the station's attendants and mechanics into one dank corner of the repair bay. There the station workers stood except one mechanic named Greer, a grease-smeared Terran who was changing the lubricant of one of the Warbirds. Well, the motto did say, "Service while you wait."

Schizophrenic leaned cross-armed against a wall. He supervised the hostages with Lefty's threatening eyes and Righty's best attempt at looking threatening. Lefty caught a mechanic trying to sneak off, so he fired a warning shot through the guy's scalp. "Any of you other idea exiles feel like sneaking off?"

"You tell 'em, Schizo," Master Asinine said. "Especially the guy with his pants on inside out."

"You're looking in a mirror, ludicrator." Lefty shifted the toothpick in his mouth with his tongue.

"Oh." Master Asinine squared his stance with the mirror and straightened his collar. "Looking good."

"Stop drinking mouthwash."

A two-person camera crew, summoned unwittingly to the station to broadcast the callout and chronicle the saga, huddled on the outskirts of the tight crowd. The floating camera eagle-eyed the gripping action that was Master Asinine.

Asinine shuffled toward the desk area of the station with Lieutenant IQ 23, Braindead, and Convenient Victim following. "Whah. These chemical fumes." Asinine exaggeratedly blinked twice to clear the fog from his brain, rubbing his running nose. "They're giving me a high. Wow, my mental faculties are impaired."

"Sir, shall I take over until you've had time to come out of your chemical delirium?" Lieutenant IQ 23 asked.

"That won't be necessary, Lieutenant. I do a lot of things with my mental faculties impaired."

Braindead had bound Convenient Victim with a magnetic towline that stretched from a device on Braindead's arm to a pair of shackles locked around both of Convenient Victim's hands. Braindead moved, and the towline forced Convenient Victim to follow and issue a feeble yelp. Master

Asinine chuckled whenever Braindead yanked his wrist randomly to jolt their prisoner. Almost as fun as pulling Convenient Victim's tail.

"Ow," Convenient Victim whined. With barely mustered eye contact, he asked Master Asinine, "C-can you please s-stop him from doing that? It's disrespectful."

"That's precisely why he does it," Asinine said in a what-else-would-you-expect-you-village-idiot tone.

Schizophrenic smacked Convenient Victim's cheek. "There's no way you could be the guy who forced literal corn up his enemies' cornholes."

Asinine tapped his foot to the beat of a Dreamboat Boys album he had playing in the background. One of them— Joey, Johnny, Jaroslav, or whatever his name was—belted out an especially high note. Asinine sang along, "Hearts aren't for playing / they're for be-ee-eating—and sometimes Valentine's Day clip art and stuff."

He looked outside. The front windows cast shadows that spilled across him. The exterior of the complex offered only an empty recharge bay that contained eight modules and a thruster charger. Other than that, Asinine had found nothing of interest. Then again, there was that tumbleweed wheeling past the station.

And where were those Intergalactic Protection pansies? Was punctuality too troublesome for them? Were they picking out each other's blouses? Master Asinine couldn't wait until those milksops arrived. The Bad Guys would blow those freaks away with their new spread-shot Face Blitzkriegs and then go for pie.

Ooh, his Face Blitzkrieg. Get this. It now fired a spread shot, a crackling ripple that spread outward toward its target. Ten times the fun. Those idiots wouldn't know what hit them: either the pulse of the Face Blitzkriegs or their own disjointed limbs. Master Asinine armed himself with a modified, twenty-six-shot 'Krieg instead of the measly sixteen-shot one. What could those IP toddlers do about it? Arrest him at the end of the battle? Maybe if their arms remained attached. But how could they withstand the attack *or* the threat of the Face Blitzkrieg superlaser? And they remained unaware of Asinine's secret weapon. So grievous, so awesome, so wired with sugar. All master plans needed a secret weapon. That was what made a plan into a *master* plan. That was the accepted law, and Master Asinine respected it.

He checked the watch he'd found in the trash. Ten minutes past Cosmonaut Chimp's tail. Where was Legion?

The familiar whoosh of an engine, the distant thunder of approaching thrusters. Master Asinine peered up as if the clamor had come from the flickering overhead lamp. Why couldn't these heathens of advancement at least invest in some light panels?

The sound rocketed closer, still closer, and stopped above the station. It ebbed into a warbling levitation noise that sounded like the hum of a master computer. A transport hovered overhead.

"MASTER ASININE, YOU UNDER ARREST FOR THE RECKLESS 'DANGERMENT O' MY DAY OFF AN' US GOOD GUYS ARE HERE T' GIVES YA A BOOT T' THE HEAD—"

———————

"Give me that!" Legion snatched the public address microphone from Jeff's grip and slapped a hand over its mouthpiece. "It's not your day off, we aren't here to arrest him for endangering it, and we're certainly not calling ourselves the Good Guys!"

"C'mon, Mustard! How come not?"

"Because you're ridiculous. Now let me handle this." He eagle-eyed the young recruit, who returned to the passenger section. He uncovered the microphone, trying to figure out what was scarier: that Jeff knew the words *reckless endangerment* or that the police were the ones who'd taught them to him. At least Jeff had stopped pronouncing it as "engenderment" or, right now, Lowensland would be thinking something entirely different.

———————

"Reckless endangerment of their day off?" Master Asinine stood by the window, a curl in his lip. "Lieutenant, what the crock is that?"

"I'm checking *The Big Book of Trumped-Up Charges* as we speak, sir." Lieutenant IQ 23's gaze stayed bound to the datasheet he held just below his chest. He flipped through its information with page-turning hand gestures. It was good to see him so often use his birthday present. Braindead stared over his shoulder like a high school student indiscreetly cheating on a final exam.

The megaphone boomed again, but this time the voice was one Asinine recognized. "GEORGE LOWENSLAND, THIS IS LIEUTENANT COLONEL MATROSS LEGION OF INTERGALACTIC PROTECTION. FOR YOUR HOSTAGE-RELATED CHARGES AND PAST TRANSGRESSIONS AGAINST THE PLANETARY UNION OF RENOVODOMUS, WE HAVE COME TO PLACE YOU UNDER ARREST. TURN YOURSELF AND YOUR FOLLOWERS IN."

Oh boy. Master Asinine rubbed his hands together. An urge to dance accompanied his sinister laugh. Now for the action-packed showdown.

This called for a celebration. "Braindead, yank your wrist back." To the tune of a strangled "gah," Asinine snatched his Face Blitzkrieg from the tool bench where he had earlier left it. He approached the front garage and pressed his cheek against a window to peer up at the transport in which those Good Guys—or whatever Legion called them—had arrived. Only an overcast shadow was visible, which spilled from the roof and over the recharge bay.

"Shall I give them a good knock of the Face Blitzkrieg, sir?" Lieutenant IQ 23 stood ready behind him.

"No," Asinine said after a moment of thought. "You shall acquire me a Kit Kat from the candy machine."

"Ah. Your thinking snack, sir." In the windowpane, the reflection of IQ 23's finger gently wrapped around the trigger of his Face Blitzkrieg. "I'll acquire that candy bar with extreme prejudice."

"The only kind of acquisition I like, Lieutenant," Master Asinine said.

Lieutenant IQ 23's padded footsteps marked his trek to the lounge. Braindead's reflection followed with Convenient Victim's in tow, which made Asinine wonder why grabbing a snack took a team of three.

Asinine pressed his cheek more firmly against the window. He still couldn't spot anything past the recharge station's eave.

"WILL YOU RESPOND, LOWENSLAND?" Legion's voice through the megaphone rattled the windows. What a chump.

"Of course I'll respond," Master Asinine said to himself. "I'm just figuring out how many shots to respond *with*." He backed away from the windows to check the cowering mechanics and whimpering station attendants. Well, they weren't cowering or whimpering. They were standing, chatting, and distributing coffee and creamers. Apparently Asinine's reputation for laid-back hostage situations/tea parties preceded him. But once they tasted the blitzkrieg of their faces, he'd *make* them cower and whimper. Especially if those Good Guys refused to shut off that jackhammer engine. It was driving him nuts.

He pointed at one hostage with his Face Blitzkrieg. "You there, with the arms. Come here." He gestured the hostage forward by sweeping his pistol toward himself. The Terran he'd selected must have been the one previously changing his lubricant (and removing the empty Space Cow fast-food bags from underneath the seats) because his shirt breast showed "Greer" embroidered on his nametag in cursive lettering.

Greer rolled his eyes and placed his coffee cup on Master Asinine's shiny Warbird's nose cone—had he no respect? That thing was a *classic*! Asinine winced when the cup's grip scuffed the Warbird's finish.

Greer strolled toward him and chewed a sliver off an oiled fingernail, his hair gelled back with grease. "What is it?" He chewed the fingernail as if it were bubblegum.

Asinine stumbled back a step. "What *is* it, Mr. Attitude? What it *is* is things are about to get hairy. That's what it is. I want you to go outside"—for emphasis, Asinine tapped Greer's chest with his Face Blitzkrieg—"and tell those Good Guys up there to land before their engine's hum splits my head in two."

Something stirred outside the front garage window. Asinine looked out and…Oh, great. He gasped, watching a Terran—flying under his own hyperability, no less—drop into sight and swoop toward him. The window disintegrated into glittering shards, not because the Terran youth had struck it but because he had shot it with light from his fingertips!

"I'm gonna mess ya up like a nuclear blam from a power plant!" the youth chirped over the crash of the pelting glass.

The sucker who called himself Power Plant swooped

toward Master Asinine. Asinine shoved Greer away and fired a Face Blitzkrieg ripple at the sucker. In a discharge of static energy, the ripple crackled and surrounded Power Plant, misguiding the air current on which he rode. The blond youth slammed into the ceiling and dropped to the oily ground with a muffled grunt.

"How'd you like that?" Asinine kicked him with a hearty rib tickler.

Power Plant stayed down. He struggled to lift himself off the floor but was too banged up. Being banged up was usually the effect of having your body slammed against a concrete ceiling, and then dropped eight feet onto a concrete floor. Asinine knew that from his many excursions to water parks. He silently congratulated himself and looked up through the shattered front window…

…at the five columns of laser rope that dropped to the ground. Finally! His body tingled from watching the columns sway in the wind.

One of those Good Guys dropped down each rope. Legion hung on the center rope with one arm entwined and the other holding his precious Marsek pistol.

"Lowensland!" Legion leveled his pistol at Asinine before the generics could react or even hurry out of the lounge where they served jelly-filled doughnuts and warm herbal tea to the hostages. "I'm placing you under arrest, you murderous piece of slime!"

Master Asinine thought quickly. He had to or else he'd

end up in prison or splattered against the back wall. He parried left. Legion's gun erupted in a torrent of light-bullets that struck the wall behind Asinine. The wall exploded in a slamdance of debris. Asinine hit the ground, slid away, and hopped to his feet. He caught a glimpse of the camera crew and station workers dodging through a rusty back door.

Oh, just great. There went the hostages. All but that one who kept asking for spare moolahs. He was probably waiting to pilfer Asinine's moolahs, but no way would Asinine give them up since it was laundry night and the laundromat was expensive. Accursed currency, lording it over his wardrobe.

"I'll handle these chumps." Schizophrenic vaulted over Asinine and dodged to avoid a volley of light-bullets. He fired, almost striking one of Legion's patsies in the neck. He leaped back and landed behind the front desk, and then ducked to avoid pieces of the oak top that blew apart in chunks from a rain of light-bullets. Sporadically, he sprang up to fire at the Good Guys, keeping them from infiltrating the repair bay. Burned wood scented the room with each round he fired.

He ducked back down. "Hey, you wannabe wannabes, a little help here!" A hand emerged and splattered the storefront with more light-bullets.

"Sir!" Lieutenant IQ 23 hurried around one corner, reappearing from wherever this arcane candy dispenser hid. Braindead and Convenient Victim followed.

"You, come here. *Now.*" Master Asinine pointed at Convenient Victim. All tension in Convenient Victim's body loosened to nothing. He approached with uneven steps. When he reached Asinine, Asinine jabbed the barrel of his Face Blitzkrieg against his chin. "I want you in that front-desk area, drawing fire away from Schizophrenic. Got that? Braindead, release him."

Convenient Victim shuddered. He stepped back and stumbled over a crack in the floor. "N-no. Please."

Braindead deactivated the towline. Convenient Victim's eyes bulged at Master Asinine so intently he'd beat a hypnotist's audience in a staring contest. He swallowed audibly and began a short stumble to the station's front desk. Master Asinine wondered if the door out there was locked. Or if he'd remembered to take his banana-nut muffins out of the oven back at home. Crock, what a waste of a whole sleeve of muffin cups and whatever the resulting fire ate.

Another window detonated into glass snow in front of Convenient Victim. He startled back when one of Legion's simpletons entered with hands pointed forward and red hair blazing in the light.

"Convenient Victim!" The simpleton reached the blue-skinned milksop and forced him down with a kick to the abdomen. Convenient Victim released a yelp that was drowned out when the simpleton said, "I represent Intergalactic Protection, and I'm placing you under arrest for treason and past transgressions against the planetary union of Renovodomus." The redhead dropped onto Convenient Victim and pinned the wimp's chest underneath a knee. "And somebody shut off that horrible boy-band clamor."

The redhead retrieved a thumbnail-sized device from an arm pouch and slapped it onto Convenient Victim's forehead. The milksop's limbs slackened to the ground. The device must have been one of those semiparalysis chips. Finally some coolness graced this throwback recharge station.

More IP lapdogs jumped through the shattered front windows. Asinine retreated from the melee into the repair bay. Lieutenant IQ 23 and Braindead followed him to the hall that led to the storage room. To IQ 23, Asinine said, "Distract the Good Guys. I've got to ready the secret weapon and beat my old high score on the *Frogger* machine in the basement."

"Show that computerized traffic who's boss, sir." Lieutenant IQ 23 and Braindead retreated toward the garage.

Legion watched Jeff lift himself off the floor with his fingers spread and his breathing labored. Jeff managed to get onto all fours, hunched over as if having vomited.

Legion helped brace Jeff to lift him up. "Are you okay?"

Jeff mustered a nod. Legion had seen worse. Good. No casualties so far. Should he call his troop to the sidelines, out of danger? He bit his lip. No. He had to learn to trust them, or Sopher's sacrifice would be squandered and Lowensland would win. He hurried past Jeff into the repair bay.

Something cut the air above his head. He ducked. With the sound of disturbed wind, a sword swung around for another attack. The move was unpracticed, sloppy. Legion dropped and kicked the swordsman's kneecap.

The swordsman bellowed and released his weapon to clutch his knee. Legion stood, grabbed the swordsman's collar, and slammed him against a plastiwood room divider. The divider swayed, threatening to peel into slivered planks. Legion examined his attacker, the Terran so often in Asinine's accompaniment whom Patton had said was media-named Lieutenant IQ 23. He wore hard-plastic armor and a mask concealing his identity but not his lack of fashion sense. Whose bright idea was it to attach question marks to his mask's temples? Probably Lowensland's. Nobody else would collect so many garish colors in this head-to-toe quilt.

Legion heard movement behind him but couldn't check because he still held the swordsman against the wobbling divider. A gun clicked. He felt the sound scrape his ear.

Boom! For a moment, Legion thought he had died—but no. He looked back at Reef and a Virillian pushing against each other, both grappling a Face Blitzkrieg above their heads. Behind the skirmish sat a drooling, semiparalyzed Convenient Victim. Drunkenly, Convenient Victim stumbled to stand, the device on his teal-colored forehead debilitating most of his movement.

Whatever hyperability Reef possessed, he wasn't using it against this swordsman. Reef kicked, kicked again, and the Virillian collapsed. Legion was surprised Reef could kick at all. He seemed like a great strategist, but he'd raised Legion's suspicions when he'd mentioned recovering from whiskey addiction a few times. He'd raised them more when mentioning his favorite drink was whiskey with a twist of Scotch.

Legion looked back at the swordsman he still held against the wall and—

He ducked. The swordsman's freed hand held a Face Blitzkrieg from which he fired a ripple of bent reality. The undulation glowed in bright blue, floating toward Reef.

"Reef!" Legion knocked the struggling swordsman back with a punch to the nose. "Heads up! Not literally!"

Reef looked up—ducked aside! Convenient Victim looked up as well. Scared, shocked, dazed. Whatever the reason, he reacted too slowly. The Face Blitzkrieg warbled through his neck. It pushed his throat back in a wavelet of distorted space and surged into the Warbird behind him. The Warbird's side panel twisted into a misshapen corkscrew and slammed onto the cement floor. The ripple crunched its repair-bay supports into metallic mulch.

The crackling static energy sizzled out. Convenient Victim choked on a knotted throat, a deformed wad of fused tissue and organs extruding through skin that was darkened to a navy blue from its previous teal. Bright orange acid sprayed from a hole in spurts. He clutched at the tangle of flesh of his neck and tipped backward. His head struck the Warbird, snapped off, and rolled down his chest.

Legion slapped the Face Blitzkrieg from the swordsman's hand. The pistol spun across the ground and bounced against Convenient Victim's body. "Reef, take care of this second-stringer." Legion threw the swordsman aside. "I need to stop Lowensland from using that thing's big brother on the entire planet."

With the Virillian unconscious, Reef grabbed the swordsman by the neck and backhanded him. "That twisted side panel is coming out of your allowance, young man."

Legion snatched up the Face Blitzkrieg. He grabbed his Marsek from his hip holster. Two guns? No. He'd keep one hidden. He slid the Face Blitzkrieg into the holster and kept the Marsek out. Slowly, he sidestepped toward the door through which Lowensland had escaped. His heart raged like a piston. His legs bowed like flat tires. What if Lowensland was watching around the corner with another Face Blitzkrieg?

He tapped two fingers on the grip of his Marsek, a habit from old military days. He reached the door. It slid open, and he slipped through, pivoted left, and thrust his Marsek forward. Nothing but a long, narrow hallway with one light bulb swinging lazily on a rusty chain. No doors or windows led out except one shut door at the end of the hallway and the door through which he'd come. The wall on the right had cracked and a shred of wallpaper hung flaccidly from it. More and more, this recharge station looked condemned.

Legion tiptoed through the hall, stretching his stride as far as he could. Fright usually slowed him, but at least the recharge station had no pointless l-tech gadgetry. Nevertheless, Lowensland could be hiding behind the door with a Face

Blitzkrieg.

Legion reached the door. Stress-caused liver splotches littered his forehead. He shook. Those splotches were probably growing.

He slowly reached for the access panel in his moist palm. The access panel looked dilapidated: smeared with dirt and cracked in several places, it revealed peeled wires and rusted springs aching to burst out. And the door was hinged. Hinged doors were absent except in rundown areas. Lowensland was probably going out of his mind over the lack of technology here.

Legion's finger slid greasily over the access panel and tapped its button. The door unlatched with a squeak. He pushed it open, first with a nudge…and then a kick!

The door swung away, smashed against the wall, and bounced back. "George Lowensland, by order of Intergalactic Protec—" *Bang!* The door slammed shut against Legion's nostrils.

He blinked. Blinked again.

Stupid door. He reached for the panel, tapped its button, and pushed lightly. "George Lowensland, by order of Intergalactic Protection, I'm placing you under arrest."

The room looked like a storage area, dusty shelves along its walls and broken machinery occupying the back half. The thick air felt grimy and smelled faintly of chemicals and dust. Lowensland stood in the room's center, next to a scuffed metal crate. At least ten feet tall, the crate's front was stenciled with the words "Secret Weapon. Open Only at Very Intense Fight. This Side Up." Somehow, Lowensland's new costume looked even more garish in person than on that viewscreen broadcast.

Legion's suction fingertips felt like claws, and he itched to pluck out Lowensland's eyes.

"Legion, behold!" Tensely, Lowensland's raised left hand gripped the air. His teeth were clamped so tightly that his jaw muscles bulged, threatening to snap his incisors into shards. His oafish smirk extended beyond the normal bounds of any Terran mouth, the only thing on Lowensland that exceeded normal bounds.

Legion watched Lowensland's mad-scientist expression redden into the color of raw hamburger. When Lowensland said nothing, Legion asked, "Behold what?"

"My secret weapon!" Lowensland's face remained dementedly contorted. Had he popped some blood vessels?

Legion tilted his head. "What secret weapon? That's a crate. Come on. Let's hurry this along. Don't make me ask any more questions. And don't hold your breath. You're turning purple."

Lowensland spat the last gulp of air from his lungs and tugged in a series of fatigued huffs, supporting himself with one hand on the metal crate. "Good. I was blacking out." He wiped drool from the corner of his mouth and caught his breath.

He stood, his back as erect as a surfboard. "Behold my

secret weapon." He slapped the side of the crate, which caused a blinking control panel under his hand to fire to life with numbered buttons that lit green. The front panel of the crate folded downward at a hinged crease that appeared where it had seemed there was none. The crate opened with a droning whir.

After the panel folded out into a short ramp to complete its descent, Legion stepped back. The shadow of some ominous creature shuffled in the darkness of the crate, its only illumination a pair of red triangles seven feet off the ground. Legion watched the triangles glint and then darken to crimson. The creature snorted and stepped forward to reveal its muscular, gray-skinned body. Those red triangles were its eyes.

Legion collapsed like a marionette whose puppeteer had released its strings. He grappled at his necklace with a shaky hand that had trouble clasping it. *Alaphus, please protect me,* he prayed.

The monster was part gargoyle. Below the sinister eyes sprouted a snout that breathed puffs of smoke. Two fangs curved up in hungry crescents with drool trickling from them. From its shoulder blades unfolded two majestic wings. It stepped—no, *thundered*—out of the confines of the undersized crate. Each hand and foot wielded three talons, two pointing upward and one down. The gargoyle clambered out on mammoth appendages, its tail beating the air with the sound of whipping wind breaching the silence.

It was also part humanoid. Its arms were as thick as

cannons, each leg as solid as a missile. Naked, prepared to crush unwelcome strangers, the monster possessed no genitalia, only eyes so domineering they seemed to account for half its mass.

"Behold the indestructible might of…Appetite!" Lowensland finished his announcement, strutting in self-satisfaction. He held both arms stretched out to indicate the impossible monster that stood upright to a height of about nine feet.

Legion's eyes seemed to bulge cartoonishly from their sockets. His heart dropped into his stomach and he almost released the contents of his bladder. He squeezed his necklace's cross and wished he had time to pray again before the thing stomped forward and loomed over him with such hatred he thought its eyes might blast radioactive beams.

"Appetite, destroy the interloper." Lowensland marched forward with the creature. "And be quick about it. I have a pile of dirty dishes at home and no machine to clean them for me unless I learn how to use a dishwasher."

The gargoyle reached out with one gargantuan claw— Legion ducked aside—and it grabbed…it grabbed something. A contraption rotting in the corner of the room. Appetite yanked its arm back, and the object it had grabbed released a metallic shriek. The gargoyle drew a twisted fragment to its jaws and slammed the fragment into its gigantic mouth.

Appetite grabbed another handful of the contraption. The contraption suffered from so much dilapidation that dust rose from it. Legion dropped his hands and stood. He almost raised his Marsek but thought he no longer needed it against this preoccupied creature.

Lowensland looked at Legion with a shrug. "Well, I guess you get what you pay for. If Appetite had half a brain, it'd be eating you right now. As things stand, it has an attention problem."

"This is your secret weapon? Don't you have a screening process for things like this?"

"Well, it's eating something. At least *look* scared."

"Fine."

"Good. Now, if you don't mind, I have a territorial treaty to sign with the gang from GWAR, and if I show up late, they'll find creative ways to use kitchen utensils on my insides and floss their teeth with my intestines. I swear I'll never look at salad tongs the same way again." He shuddered. "At least they have commendable dental hygiene."

Lowensland seized his Face Blitzkrieg from his pouch and pointed it at Legion, at the same time whipping a device out of his pocket. A fob with a single orange button. "So let's just skip to the part where I show the public just what I can do." He jabbed his thumb over the button. "This'll show IP not to laugh at me."

"Lowensland, what did you just do?" Legion's legs twitched. He wanted to dive for Lowensland, grab the fob, but Lowensland reasserted his aim.

The fob glowed and, from a speaker on its underside, a

voice said, "Superlaser activated. Energy charge commencing. Please wait."

Lowensland regarded the fob with astonishment. "It has to charge first? What a rip-off! We can land a man on all forty-seven moons, but we can't come up with a superlaser that's good to go when you need it. What, am I preheating an oven here?"

Legion felt his body grow icy. "You activated your superlaser? But you're standing on this planet! You'll blitzkrieg your own face along with everyone else's. Did I just say that out loud?"

"The real issue with weapons nowadays is their charge times."

"Four minutes until face blitzkriegification," the fob said.

Lowensland squeezed the fob. "But that'll take us into tomorrow." He jabbed the button—

"Superlaser deactivated."

"Oh, great. I just shut the thing off. I really have to tell my tech guys that not everything has to be a toggle switch." Lowensland jabbed the button again to reactivate his weapon.

"This can't happen, Lowensland." Legion dived for the fob, but Lowensland snatched it aside and fired his Face Blitzkrieg. Legion dropped and rolled. His Marsek fell out of his sweaty grip and clattered away. The Face Blitzkrieg's ripple sailed past him so closely that he felt air push against him.

Legion vaulted forward, knocking the Face Blitzkrieg

and the fob from Lowensland's hand. The fob spun into a corner across the room.

Legion drew his own Face Blitzkrieg. The weapon ricocheted off Lowensland's slap. It spun away and crashed against a wall. Legion prepared to lunge for it—

A meaty paw slammed over the weapon. Appetite brought the Face Blitzkrieg up and tossed it into its maw. The beast began chewing with the hungry sound of smacking lips.

Legion knew he ought to take cover. The Face Blitzkrieg could explode in the monster's mouth. Too shocked, he instead stared at Appetite, who chomped on diodes and torn wires that ejected from its maw like mush from a baby's mouth. It swallowed and then lumbered into another corner in search of more fodder.

An electronic voice spoke over the lip smacking, "Three minutes until face blitzkriegification."

Something smacked Legion's chin. He hit the floor and slammed against a mangled machine the Face Blitzkrieg's ripple had hit. A perverse creation now, the machine lay in a display of random entanglements. Legion stood. He supported himself on a bent bar that jutted from the useless box. His sweat-coated hand slipped on the nub. He looked up—

Like a lumberjack chopping wood, Lowensland swung with a disconnected plumbing pipe. Legion tore his bent bar out and held it aloft. Lowensland's pipe clanged against the bar, the reverberation shaking through Legion's forearms. Legion heaved backward against the twisted machine.

Lowensland's pipe struck his bar again, barely above his fingers.

"Two minutes until face blitzkriegification."

"You're not killing anymore, Lowensland." Legion dodged to avoid Lowensland's hard swing on the machine. The machine gasped in a cloud of smoke, its last ounce of life now spent. Legion kicked Lowensland in the stomach—tried to duck around him to retrieve the fob but Lowensland blocked him. He parried right and swung. Lowensland recovered—blocked at chest level.

There the two struggled with weapons forced against one another, each trying to drive the other down.

"Join me, Legion." Lowensland spat his words out between grunts.

Legion's face contorted. "What?" Was Lowensland offering a deal? Did he actually think Legion would accept?

"Join me. Together we'll rule the cosmos. *Both* of us— as kings. Or at least bishops."

"Never," Legion said, panting.

"Wait wait wait. Before you answer, let me say just one word that will change your mind drastically." Amusement played across Lowensland's face. "Marsupials."

"Huh? Marsupials?" Legion let falter some of his strength, so Lowensland countered by releasing some of his own. They separated.

Lowensland caught his breath. "Marsupials. You know, a mammal with a—"

"I know what a marsupial is. We have them on my home planet, too. How are marsupials supposed to change my mind?"

"I'm talking insane marsupials. Destructive cyber-kangaroos with the killing potential of a hundred normal ones, laying waste to countless innocents. Kanga-destruction the likes of which Renovodomus has never seen. Marsupials. This idea is way more practical than my idea of infinite monkeys with infinite munitions factories. It's so boring in this galaxy. All I want is to make things crazy fantastic. Also to break lots of stuff."

"Like how you suggested it would be more exciting if everyone were on fire?"

"Okay, remember that idea was better considering my public healthcare plan."

"Forget it. I'd rather team up with *that* thing." Legion thumbed the colossal Appetite, who grabbed a chunk of another decrepit machine with both paws and tossed that chunk into its mouth.

"One minute until face blitzkriegification."

"Then cyber-dragocorns? They're like unicorns and dragons mixed up except they have horns for eyes, and they have horns for ears, and they fart fire."

"Stop combining animals!"

"Then no to the cyber-Labradoodles?"

"How about cyber-nothing!"

Lowensland shrugged. "Suit yourself. Hold on.

Appetite, bad boy! If you dismantle the machine, you need to eat it all. No spreading it around the room so it looks like less than it really is. I know all the tricks. I tried them myself when I was your age...whatever age you are." Appetite gave the vague impression it was paying attention.

Legion tapped the end of his bar against the floor. "Are you finished?"

"Yeah." Lowensland swung his pipe—hit Legion's ribs. Legion fell with a volt of pain flickering through his side. Lowensland kicked Legion's bar away, and it rolled to Appetite's feet.

"Energy charge concluded," the fob said, still sitting in the corner. "Commencing face blitzkrieging in alphabetical order. Please stand by."

"Alphabetical order?" Legion tried to stand, but his vision still swam, and his side still felt as if something inside had shattered. "Aaron, take cover!"

An unearthly caterwaul, like that of a tortured cat, shrieked through the door.

"Aaron!"

"No, no, don't worry." Lowensland looked unconcerned. "That's probably my generic, Aardwern. His parents had a weird obsession with alphabetization. He should probably warn his brother, Aardzvich." He paused to allow the howl to subside, but it seemed endless. Aardwern broke his ghastly wail to gurgle in a breath and then continued. "Really raising the bar on agony, isn't he?"

Legion's vision blurred, returned, blurred again. He discerned only Lowensland, who tossed his pipe aside and reached for the remaining Face Blitzkrieg. Finally the scene resolved to reveal Lowensland standing over him, sick determination in his expression.

"Moving onto people whose names begin with *aardz*," the fob said.

Lowensland clicked his tongue. "Well, that's that for Aardwern."

"Get this over with already." Legion braced a hand on his knee.

"Can't wait for *L*, can you? Well, I'll have to use the portable version on you." Lowensland pointed the Face Blitzkrieg at Legion. "I'm going to enjoy this."

Legion stared up at Lowensland with venom burning his throat. "Like you enjoyed killing Sopher?"

A clang! A spark rang out, and the Face Blitzkrieg burst apart. One half clattered to the floor and smashed against an empty box, the other half remaining in Lowensland's grip. Legion's eyes scrambled around for an answer and caught someone in the doorway.

Jeff stood there with his left hand aimed forward in the form of a child's make-believe handgun. A trail of serpentine smoke rose from his fingertips. "Put th' spankomatic away."

"Power Plant!" Lowensland tossed aside the remains of his weapon.

"Media name ain't Power Plant. It's Grandmaster

Awesome…uhm…" His posture loosened and he trailed off. "X…R…somethin' somethin'. Crock, spellin' numbers is tough. Okay, so we gonna *makes* it Power Plant." He shoved his play gun forward again and his resolute posture returned. But a chewing noise from the corner of the room diverted his attention. Without turning from Lowensland, he jabbed his chin at Appetite. "What's wit' the hungry, hungry hippo eatin' all that wall? Can I plays wit' it?"

Legion nodded no. "Jeff, hungry, hungry hippos aren't toys. They're secret weapons. Apparently."

"Name's Jeffy. Can't nobody gets any o' my names right?"

"Continuing onto people whose names begin with *aaro*." The fob seemed happy with its progress.

Legion scrambled to grab the fob—scooped it up from the dusty floor—squashed his thumb over the button.

"Genocide deactivated."

Legion melted against the wall, realizing his thirsty lungs hadn't tasted air since he'd dived for the fob. Now he hyperventilated, easing his shoulder against the wall's mottled concrete. He dropped the fob and, with a firm step, ground his heel into it. It burst apart, tendrils of wires spewing out.

And then came the low-toned beeps that were so background, so white noise they had escaped Legion's notice until now. Like the signals of transports undulating on a radarscope, the beeps nudged Legion's ears and forced him to pay heed. He stood. He followed the beeps…tracked them…

drew closer…grew annoyed at Lowensland screaming, "Warmer, warmer, hot…hot…*scolding hot!*" He reached the crate from which Appetite had emerged.

He looked inside and swore he heard a smile crackle across Lowensland's sinister lips. A beeping bomb hid inside the crate, fashioned out of a digital alarm clock from ancient times. Its countdown reached a minute and forty-four seconds. Oh, no.

Legion gawked at the crate. "What is with you and timers?"

"I knew you'd come looking for me." Lowensland chuckled. "And I was determined to have that bomb waiting when you arrived."

"This thing's set to explode in less than two minutes!"

"Oh." Lowensland opened his mouth and, for only a moment, paused before saying, "Guess my calculations were off. Well, that sucks."

Legion grabbed Jeff's shoulders. "Find the others, get out of here!" He turned to Lowensland. "I'll finish off this murderer."

"But you dies if ya sticks around. Might not be good."

"I don't care—as long as this madman gets what's coming. You need to leave." Legion shoved Jeff away, but Jeff grabbed his wrist. Legion reared back a fist. "Let go, Jeff. I have a madman to kill."

"Uh-uh. Ya stays, ya dies. I gonna holds my breath till you gets comin.'" Jeff gulped back a lungful of oxygen.

"If I *don't* stay, I'll never be able to live with myself!" Legion grappled at Jeff's hand around his wrist, the beeping getting louder and louder. "Lowensland needs a colossal beating even if it costs me my life."

"I'm that important!" Lowensland thumbed himself.

And then Patton's voice. *Again.* At the worst times. "Control your resentment"—Legion had given up on that a long time ago—"or it will jeopardize everyone." And then, for some reason, "Pick up fish oil supplements on the way home and drop off your dry cleaning."

Legion looked at Jeff, who stood stalwart. He was jeopardizing Jeff right now. He stopped struggling and stole a final glance at Lowensland, who was simultaneously scratching his ear and jerking his leg like a contented dog. "You're right." He said this not to Jeff but to Patton. "Let's go. I have to live to see my dry cleaning through to the end."

Jeff exhaled and hugged Legion's waist. "Hol' tight." A cloudburst exploded under his feet and he lifted upward. With the skill of an expert pilot, he maneuvered through the door, sailed through the hallway, and curved into the repair bay.

Jacob and Reef stood ahead. Mark, Ghiglix, Everett, and Aaron prodded some captured Bad Guys into a large jail transport. It was not an Intergalactic Protection jail-tran. Local law enforcement had summoned it.

Jeff and Legion landed. The hostages had already escaped, so Legion hurried through his short speech for the sake of his own troops. "Listen up, everyone. Get this jail-tran as far away as possible. There's a bomb set to explode in about fifteen seconds. We need to clear out *now*!"

Master Asinine couldn't die. Not now. He was so close to ruling at the top rung of the criminal ladder, so far from being kicked around at the bottom of the military stool.

He had somehow enticed Appetite toward the bomb, away from the snack it was making out of an old medical kit it had retrieved from a locked cabinet. Well, locked until it had eaten the lock. It now stared vapidly at the bomb, speculating whatever its low-watt, two-celled brain speculated on occasions like this. Maybe something as complex as addition.

"Eat the bomb," Master Asinine said. Gentle shoves weren't urging Appetite, so he pushed harder, still unable to budge the animal. The bomb beeped its seventeenth-to-last second. "Come on, you degenerate beast. Last week you clean out my vitamin drawer, and today you're on a hunger strike?"

Asinine climbed into the crate. Maybe the snooze button would add ten minutes to the timer. He pressed the red square in one corner of the clock. Huh. Maybe it wouldn't. The counter reached nine seconds so he climbed out.

Well, Appetite was indestructible. So had said the mail-order catalog. Master Asinine circled around the gargoyle, hopped onto its Herculean shoulders, and ducked behind its head when the final digital glimmer counted the last second.

He hoped this would be a short ride.

The recharge station detonated behind Legion in a deafening eruption. He and Jeff shot over the street curb, the blast spewing them out and pushing them down toward the ground. If not for their impact suits, the shockwave would have shattered their bones and smeared them across the pavement.

Jeff unintentionally let go of Legion. The pavement sped closer-closer-closer-*bang*. Legion reeled across the road, side over point over side. He tumbled past the median and banged against the curb. His skin was grated in hot patches, his body lit with a searing inferno of pain. He looked up to see Jeff bounce against the pavement and collide with a parked civ-tran in a lot across the street.

Behind him, Mark, Jacob, Aaron, and the others had narrowly escaped. The backs of their impact suits flapped in the breeze, tattered and scorched.

Another explosion. In the station's charging deck, recharge module after recharge module detonated in sequence. The last explosion pushed against Legion with an unseen hand that threw him backward into the same civ-tran Jeff had hit.

Billows of ashen, pungent smoke clotted the azure sky and stung Legion's nostrils with a sensation worse than anything he felt on his body. The stench of chemicals only helped irritate his sinuses, but at least the explosions had finished. Now what remained of the recharge station roared aflame. The Flagstar, which still hovered above the station, became fodder for the climbing pyre. It dipped and was lost inside the firestorm.

Hot blood and electric zaps zigzagged across the left side of Legion's body. He stood and turned away from the heat and ashes that nipped at his eyes. "Well…there goes our ride home."

Jeff checked a strip of road rash that had shredded the upper back and shoulders of his impact suit to ribbons.

Legion wobbled around with a limp and surveyed his soldiers, who had collected near a coppice of trees beyond the street. Mark, Ghiglix, Everett, Reef, Aaron, and Jacob lined the front of a growing crowd of mesmerized spectators, the jail-tran sitting off to one side. Legion would have limped over to Jeff to thank him for the tight rescue, but Mark rushed to help him stand. The older brother assessed Jeff's injuries before giving him a tight hug.

Legion turned away. Had he let anyone die? He hesitated to ask but forced himself to blurt out, "Is everyone all right?" He had trouble raising his voice over the fiery din. Everyone responded positively.

Phew. He'd lost nobody to that dog Lowensland. And locating that superlaser wouldn't be difficult. Intergalactic Protection had probably already searched the sky for the big glowing weapon that took four minutes to power up. They were probably already determining ways to dismantle the device.

At least the success of this mission meant his discharge was lifted. And was Patton right? Was this team a good idea?

Was Legion experienced enough to lead these hyperpeople? Could he trust them to survive? Yes. He could. He resolved to worry no longer about losing another man. After all, if they had failed to act, a lot of innocents would have died today—or at least have been forced to wear feathered tutus if Lowensland's hostage demands weren't met.

Legion approached Jeff and patted his shoulder. "Hey, Jeff. Thanks for saving my life in there. I would have been cooked if you hadn't come in. I owe you."

"Owes me 'nough to calls me Jeffy, right?" Jeff's face animated.

"No." Legion offered a lifeless chuckle. "Not if my life depended on it."

Another explosion rattled the ground. A fireball belched up from the center of the station, and the canopy of the recharge pod bay collapsed with a crunch.

That haunting gunshot that had killed Sopher crackled in Legion's head. This explosion wouldn't stop Lowensland. Somehow he had survived. Legion knew it.

"Was that all in a day's work?" he asked himself. He limped away from the blazing wreckage, encrusted with a lining of rocks stuck to his hip. He dragged his reluctant right foot, his muscles protesting every movement he forced on them.

"That was amazing!" a voice said from his right. Legion lurched carefully around to find the escaped camera crew—a Terran reporter and her Virillian cameraman—directing a floating camera at Legion via hand movements.

Legion didn't acknowledge the crew. He was uninspired to do anything but sit and heal. Or die. Whichever.

"Camera rolling?" the reporter asked her cameraman, and the Virillian presented her with a scowl and an intolerant nod. "Great." The reporter whipped her hair over her shoulder and slid into the camera's frame with a microphone she shoved at her mouth. She now spoke in a fabricated British accent. "We're back live with *Viewnet News* on channel fourteen, sponsored by Lab Rat Scientific. Viewers, what you have witnessed here"—she gestured toward the firestorm in the background—"has been an act of true heroism. And here is one of those brave heroes who, moments ago, had rescued at least a dozen workers and this camera crew from the clutches of a hostage situation. Have you anything to tell our viewers?" The reporter shoved the microphone at Legion's face, startling Legion back a step.

Through a haze of pain, Legion looked down at the microphone. "Uhm, we were simply…I don't know…uh…" He stopped, looked straight into the camera, and collected his thoughts. His body flared savagely, hotter than its previous dull throb. "We were just stopping off to recharge our transport. We would also like to announce that the United Recharge Station is"—an explosion erupted, causing the station's roof to split with the snapping sound of a tree slowly toppling—"undergoing extensive renovations."

"Excellent. Brave warriors stopping to recharge their

transport, unwittingly caught in the middle of a hostage situation. You were acting under the authority of Intergalactic Protection. What do you brave warriors call yourselves?"

"The Good Guys!" yelled a distant voice from across the street. Jeff's voice. "C'mon. The Good Guys!"

"We're the…uhm…uh…" Oh, no. His group still had no title. Who were they? What media name could he give? Only one thing came to mind. He fought against it, but what else could he say? His mind had drawn nothing but a blank. What a stupid time to disengage. What was that about collecting his thoughts?

"The—Good—Guys!" Jeff was now leaping around.

Legion groaned. A feeble moron replaced the stammering idiot who'd spoken before. "We're the Good Guys."

"The Good Guys?" The reporter had dropped her accent. She hung out her tongue as if she'd tasted a putrid orange. "What kind of a media name is that? Might as well call yourselves the Wastes of Space." She gestured to her cameraman. "Rffflllxxxxxttthhh, cut the feed. Let them run repeats of last week's glacier races. We're off."

The news crew sauntered off with the Virillian signaling the camera to follow. Legion watched for no more than a few seconds before he limped toward the curb. A burn flared mercilessly up his left side.

In spite of the blasting pain, he grinned. He'd defeated Lowensland. And with no casualties. Maybe he *could* one day atone for Sopher's sacrifice. Maybe IP *could* work through him. Maybe Alaphus would even release him from IP's l-tech sponsorship death trap. But right now, he didn't want to think about that. It was time to go home. Time to take therapy seriously. Time to heal. Time to relieve himself of his grief over Sopher's death.

Time to pull this chunk of shrapnel out of his leg.

CHAPTER THIRTEEN
LOSING SUCKS

Master Asinine clung tenaciously to Appetite's back. The gargoyle sailed upward in a diagonal trajectory, oblivious to what had happened. Asinine climbed onto its shoulders and wrapped his hands around its eyes, but the thing was so stupid—so fundamentally stupid—that it didn't know or didn't care. Perhaps it wondered who had turned out the lights. Its tinfoil brain was probably trying to spark up a thought or two.

Asinine's plan was ruined. Well, maybe not ruined. At least delayed. But those Face Blitzkriegs had turned out to be a letdown.

Had to call his lieutenant for help. He tapped the pinna of his left ear where it held a pea-sized communication device. His gabber. "Gabber, acknowledge. Contact entity Lieutenant." A thin stem with a mouthpiece at its end shot out of the gabber and curled down to Asinine's lips. An earpiece curled around his head to his right ear. The bud itself became the left earpiece.

"Contacting entity Lieutenant. Seeking connection."

This brand of gabber wasn't the safest. But, ear cancer begone, he had to make the call before he sailed too high and lost consciousness.

Master Asinine cleared his throat a second before the gabber said, "Connection attained."

"Lieutenant? Hi, it's me. Not much. How about you? Good, good. Braindead and Schizophrenic okay? Good. Listen, can you swing by and pick me up? Well, somewhere between one hundred miles below and fifty miles below ozone level. Not sure exactly. How? I'm riding our secret weapon. Yeah, I—Lieutenant? Ha, ha, yes, I see how that could be funny. You do? Yeah, I'll hold. Oh, and you have my Kit Kat? Excellent."

THE END

NEXT ISSUE:
Written in Aqua-Spanish doublespeak where available.

Because you're such lovely people and your friends speak very highly of you, here's a preview of what happens next time on *Space Aliens Say the Most Horrible Slurs in Print*

In a Galaxy Far, Far AwRy
Issue 2: Home Sweet Home Invasion

When Jeff and Jacob crash-land on the Bad Guys' new home turf, a simple mission goes from routine observe-and-report duty to straight-up survival. And their new pilot, a robot with a vocal processor built from car alarms, doesn't make hiding any easier whenever it speaks its mind at 120 decibels.

Can Jeff and Jacob outwit Master Asinine's hunting party long enough for Legion and Mark to mount a rescue operation? Or will the hunting party execute them before they can raid the Bad Guy pantry?

Check www.inagalaxyfarfarawRy.com for upcoming release info…if the great apocalypse doesn't hit. If it *does* hit, you can find me in a panic, setting fire to random landmarks. It's an either-or.

CHAPTER ONE
APPROPRIATION THROUGH
SUPERCOOLOCITY

October 29, 9109. 10:13 p.m. (Galactic Standard Time).

The space station was big. But was it big enough? Ah, that wouldn't matter once Master Asinine installed the radioactive thundermammal moat. Heh. A moat surrounding a space station. He'd have to give himself November's Employee of the Month award for concocting that idea. Funny how that would make him employee of the month sixteen times in a row.

Master Asinine had found this moon-sized space station abandoned, and he had decided he had to have it. From here, the Bad Guys would launch their assault on the Good Guys, crush them, and wrest control of this galaxy. How unstoppable this station would become, how destructive its flatulence. Was *flatulence* the right word? Didn't matter. Asinine found this station more than flatulent for his purposes.

The station had been vacated by Virillian scientists who had used it to study cancerous growths on asparagus or some such scientific money pit. The Bad Guys' head scientist, Brick, claimed it was the last of seventeen space stations used to terraform the planet Vesta into a habitable planet—a venture later deserted—but Brick was always long winded, so Asinine usually ignored him.

The station now sat lifelessly in space. It could escape Vesta's orbit and become a free-floating ball of Bad Guy destruction. But repositioning this monster was complicated: deorbiting was impossible without initiating separation procedures with Vesta so that Vesta's planetary mainframe could compensate for the lack of counterbalanced gravity. That would alert authorities of the station's unauthorized use before Asinine unveiled his Rampage-o-Tron. But Brick would handle that mundane detail. Brick specialized in mundanity. He also specialized in freaking Master Asinine out with seventeen-syllable words.

Master Asinine shuffled away from a few generics, the anonymous Bad Guy underlines all dressed in red, and made a panoramic scan and nodded approvingly at the bare room illuminated in sunlight that dazzled through the grime-smeared windows. Some of the Bad Guys stood around him in a semicircle, watching. Smelling faintly of the unwashed metal of the walls, the room had potential if not more layers of dust than a copy of Groovemaster's *Master of Grooves* album. This room could be so much: a briefing room, a sparring room, a monster truck arena.

Ooh. Trucks crossed with monsters. Duly noted.

The irresistible coolness of the space station caused Asinine's crooked smile to grow so wide it would leave stretch marks. He sensed promise here, which supercharged his blood with sweet adrenaline. Or that might have been his fifth coffee. "I like this place. I like it a lot. Let's take it. Lieutenant, this calls for a celebration. Pizza lunch for everybody."

The crowd of thirty murmured a hubbub of approval, and Lieutenant IQ 23 perked with life. "Good idea, sir. I'll see what toppings the generics want." Beside him, Braindead shuffled his weight.

Brick cleared his throat, which sounded like the rumbling of a thousand supercomputers determining what million-letter words to use for an otherwise simple statement. His every movement, his every sound in this room echoed hollowly.

Master Asinine rolled his eyes. "Brick, if you hadn't single-handedly installed solar panels on my even bigger solar panels, I would have fired you eons ago. What blither do you want to blather on about this time?"

He turned to the long-winded know-it-all and was presented with the scientist's seven-foot brownstone frame. Brick was a body of boxy bricks. A boxy upper torso connected boxy shoulders. Boxy arms had boxy hands that extended from boxy wrists and ended in boxy fingers. Boxy legs met boxy knees supported on boxy feet. A boxy head with a boxy face controlled the boxy bulk that moved like a boxy box.

"Mr. Asinine," Brick said. He was as annoying as a jackhammer thundering between Asinine's ears. "May I aspire to verbalize a contention with the assertion on your conjecture concerning this orbital dwelling? We cannot merely appropriate this edifice for our assemblage in such a technique and comportment."

Master Asinine gagged with the urge to puke his cookie cake and vanilla custard all over Brick's feet. His stomach muscles churned bile, his brain shifting from neutral to impossible gears to vainly discern words from the turkey gobble Brick tried passing off as English. Asinine wished Brick would use vocabulary that had actually been invented.

Whatever Brick had ninnered, Asinine was going to assume it had something to do with snuffing out his fun. "Let me counter your conjecture of the appropriate assemblortment technique…contertion"—a deep breath—"whatever else you said. We found this space station. We're here. No one else is. Listen, I was talking with this old buddy of mine who says this guy he plays pinochle with has a sister who lives across from that guy who was in the *Tremors* remake with Kevin Bacon's clone, who used to work at a surveying station. Anyway, this surveying clone says nobody's used this place in years. So I call squatter's rights."

"You're calling squatter's rights on a crocking space station?" Schizophrenic's left head spat a single chuckle that echoed against the naked walls. A toothpick shifted around Lefty's lips. He snorted. "That's freaking rich."

"Shouldn't we be sitting to call squatter's rights?" Righty asked. "This can be my room. That wall is where I'll hang my poster of a wall." Schizophrenic's right hand pointed at a support beam. "Where's your room going to be?" he asked Lefty.

"Mr. Asinine," Brick said, "squatter's rights is what the common populace brands an urban myth." Naysaying. Always naysaying everything. Brick had become Asinine's most useless voice of reason. The day Asinine had found this killjoy at that mad scientists' convention had been a dark one. The madder the scientist, the more insistently that scientist would try to prove his confusing intellect.

Master Asinine stomped a foot on the steel floor. "What are you talking about? Squatter's rights is as real as Sasquatches. It's how I got my first house. It's also how I got into my first argument defending the existence of squatter's rights. Besides, this place has more offensive capabilities than I know how to operate: outer-mounted fusion cannons, laser arrays, a shark pit, a snake pit, a ball pit, a lazy Susan. Appetite, don't eat that. It's full of calories."

Appetite, the Bad Guy pet gargoyle, didn't flinch from the countertop it was using as a meal.

Brick stepped toward Asinine, his each stride a rocky slam with limbs clambering together. "Though this location's pursuits are forsaken, the denizens who retain its proprietorship may aspire to wrangle against you concerning the integrity of squatter's rights."

Master Asinine tossed a hand at the impossibility of such an event. "What, you think they'll take this place back?

Bah. If they wrangle our integrity up, we'll just call squatter's rights on them."

"I fervidly offer counsel in disagreement to this methodology of electing our headquarters."

Master Asinine's face grew a scowl. His lower lip twitched, twitched again. His mouth shaped the beginnings of many inadequate, unspoken words. He spun around at IQ 23. "Lieutenant, what the hoohah is that jabberwocky jabbering about?"

"He doesn't think taking this station is a good idea, sir."

"It's the *perfect* idea!" Master Asinine spun at Brick. "It's the most perfectest idea I've had since my idea of colonizing our water supply with Sea-Monkeys. You can't beat this place. It has squash courts."

Brick raised his hands, fingers spread. He shrugged his Mount Rushmore shoulders. "Will any technique of oration deter you from this proposal?"

Asinine crossed his arms. "No, you can't have the rest of my gravy hoagie. For no one steals the hoagie of royalty. Some have called me mad. Some have called me dangerous. Some have called me Thelma, which is weird since that's not even a boy's name. But be forewarned: those same people will soon call me ruler of the galaxy. I will be King Thelma!"

"What a freaking brain-bomb," Lefty grumbled.

"But I promise you this. Now that we have this station, nothing will stand in our way. Those Good Guys are as good as toast." Asinine clutched the air, his back arched and his fingers lifted in a malicious grasp for the stars. "As sure as my name is Thelma, we will obliterate Legion and the Good Guys! And now I could go for a good slice of toast."

Lieutenant IQ 23 raised a finger: hold on. The gabber nestled inside his ear had extended a mouthpiece and earpiece around his head. "Sir, I just got a buzz from your automated mailbox. Your Masters of the Universe toy set has arrived."

Asinine's head jerked to IQ 23. "How many times must I tell you? They're not toys. They're miniature people simulations!"

To be continued like you wouldn't believe...

APPENDIX: HYPERABILITIES

General Definitions

Ability, hyper-

A special ability that allows a person to do something normally impossible (a typical hyperability), that extends a person's talent beyond normal bounds (a hypertalent), or that mutates a person's body (a hypermutation). A person gains a hyperability if he or she has a hypergland that is overexposed to stimuli. This usually happens while the person is still in the womb and usually during the second trimester. Only one in approximately one million people develops a hyperability. Hyperabilities can be hereditary though often aren't because some fluids that pass the hyperability don't enter the placenta unless the hyperability itself has modified those fluids.

Example: shooting lasers from your eyes, being able to ignore that fart your friend let out just now

Ability degeneration, hyper-

A condition where a hyperability grows less manageable over time, usually due to disease, aging, poor diet, or a sedentary lifestyle. So like your bladder control but with a sound-and-light show.

Ability Injunction, Hyper-

A treaty among multiple galaxies that prevents hyperpeople from serving in any capacity at war. The Injunction was enacted as a result of a gross misuse of a hyperability that resulted in multiple civilian deaths. The details have since been expunged due to someone confusing a CD slot as a cupholder or something like that. Don't blame him. Compact discs hadn't been used in, like, seven thousand years by the time that wizard of technology came along.

Ability poisoning, hyper-

A condition where a person's hyperability, through overuse, creates more free radicals in his or her body than the body can nullify, to the point where the hyperability causes tissue damage or death. Note that a free radical is not a hippie.

Example: Jeff Abends's control of light, if it becomes too severe, can cause sterility

Allergy, hyper-

A condition where a hyperperson's immune response overreacts to either the hormones produced by the hypergland or the effects of the hyperability itself. But what if a person is allergic to a hyperability that provides a better immune response? Think on that conundrum.

Cube, hyper-

A four-dimensional cube. Really has nothing to do with hyperabilities, but…pppffttt. Whatevs.

Elemental

A type of hyperperson. Someone who controls fire, water,

air, or naturally occurring solids like your kidney stones.

Example: Mark Abends, Jeff Abends (limited)

Energy, hyper-

The energy produced by a hyperability, sometimes charged in the hyperperson's body and stored for later use. Like a bank that's open at decent hours.

Fundamental controller

A type of hyperperson who controls one of the messenger particles that create the fundamental forces: gluons (strong nuclear force), W and Z bosons (weak nuclear force), photons (electromagnetism), and gravitons (gravity). The graviton is totally a thing in Futureland, by the way.

Example: Jeff Abends (to a degree), who can control photons of wavelengths between 564 and 589 nanometers

Gland, hyper-

A gland that secretes hormones that activate a person's hyperability. Though a hyperability can have more than one application, each hypergland can produce only one root hyperability. In other words, if you got stuck with acid vomiting, tough luck 'cause you're not getting flight, too.

Illegal combination

A gathering of either (1) one of each type of the four elementals, (2) one of each type of the four fundamental controllers, or (3) that batch of brownies you baked. Don't play dumb. You know what I'm talking about. Hand 'em over.

Example: gathering a fire elemental, a water elemental, an air elemental, and an earth elemental in the same room for a sweet party

Immunodeficiency, hyper-

A condition where a hyperperson's immune response to his or her own hyperability is reduced enough to be unable to protect that person from the effects of his or her hyperability. Essentially burning a really short candle at both ends. Sucker.

Mutation, hyper-

A hyperability that causes a physical mutation.

Example: Everett Pendleton's wings, but not your big nose or those ears that stick out

Person/People, hyper-

A person with a hyperability, even if it isn't one of the cool ones like breathing fire or having sweet X-ray vision. The first confirmed hyperperson was born on May 27, 4989. He had the hyperability to control birds, an ability heightened through the use of bread.

Example: breathing fire or having sweet—just reread the last paragraph

Phobia, autohyper-

A persistent fear of one's own hyperability or its usage. Messed up, right?

Phobia, hyper-

A persistent fear of hyperabilities or their usage. Less messed up.

Root hyperability

The base application of a hyperability. For instance, if a

hyperperson can control light, disrupt radio waves, and erase computer memory, that person's root hyperability might be electromagnetism control or being a big fat douche.

Example: Mark Abends can fly by casting heat energy away from himself, but his root hyperability is fire generation/control

Science, hyper-

The study of hyperabilities and their effects. One of those studies in school that might actually lead to a paying job.

Talent, hyper-

A hyperability that extends a normal ability found in everyone beyond normal bounds. For instance, though everyone has the ability to play the piano, a hypertalent would allow someone to play the piano perfectly with little or no practice. These people are usually called "prodigies" or "crocking showoffs."

Example: Aaron Khouri's computer expertise, the ability to get up without hitting the snooze button several times (in case you need another reason to hate cheery morning people)

Stasis, hyper-

A medicine or magnetic resonance that stops the hypergland from secreting and negates any hypergland hormones already in the bloodstream, thus nullifying a hyperability. Some hyperstasis medication also provides antioxidants to counter free radicals. The cheap hyperstasis medication might cause urinary tract infection in some people.

Staveville Hyperperson Penitentiary

A penitentiary for hyperpeople that uses hyperstasis magnetic resonance to stop the hypergland from excreting. They have a great theater program.

Team, hyper-

A team of hyperpeople. They do their thing and look good for the camera.

Thesia, Hyper-

A brand name of hyperstasis medication. Consult your doctor to see if Hyperthesia is right for you.

Trician, hyper-

A doctor who specializes in hyperpeople and hyperabilities.

Triplet hyperability

One of three hyperabilities possessed by the same person, due to that person possessing three hyperglands. Only one person in history is known to have developed triplet hyperglands, and he wasted it on predicting the outcomes of sports games.

Twin hyperability

One of two hyperabilities possessed by the same person, due to that person possessing two hyperglands. Only one in approximately one hundred million hyperpeople develops twin hyperglands. Lucky guy.

Locality

General

A hyperability that affects or is emitted from anywhere on a person's body. Fingers? Yes. Eyeballs? Yes. Toes? Lame, but yes.

Example: Mark Abends's fire generation, which can be emitted from any part of his body, including his toes

Local

A hyperability that affects or is emitted from a single organ or part of a person's body. Not to be confused with "loco hyperability," which is scrambling people's brains during a stampede or a Black Friday sale.

Example: the death glare your boss gives you when your lunch goes too long

Loco

I lied. This actually isn't a real thing. Sorry.

Regional

A hyperability that affects or is emitted from a collection of organs that work at a single function. Body odor doesn't count.

Example: heightened hearing, which affects only the ears and their related organs

---

Range

External, no range (also classified as "External, surface")

A hyperability that affects only the surface of the hyperperson's body. You can't blame your huge nose on this either. Get over it.

Example: hypermutations like those way fierce horns I mentioned before

External, range

A hyperability with a ranged effect, no matter how lame that effect is (cough, cough, making others itch, cough).

Example: telekinesis

Internal

A hyperability that affects only the inside of the hyperperson's body, your uncle Frank's acid reflux not included.

Example: Aaron Khouri's computer hypertalent, maybe your uncle Frank's acid reflux after all (it's pretty remarkable)

Mutation

A hypermutation; has no range.

Example: Everett Pendleton's wings, growing awesome horns on your forehead

---

Activation

Conscious

A hyperability that must be activated by conscious thought.

Example: Jacob Refensil's self-duplication, sarcasm if it's really funny

Constant

A hyperability that can't be switched on or off.

Example: hypermutations

Unconscious

A hyperability that activates without the hyperperson's choice or knowledge; automatic.

Example: accelerated healing, your spouse's encyclopedic knowledge of every mistake you've ever made

Master Asinine/
George Lowensland

Lieutenant IQ 23

Braindead /
Nerrgggghhhhhggg

Schizophrenic/
Lefty and Righty

Franchise/
Jacob Refensil

Power Plant/
Jeff Abends

Momentum/
Ghiglix

Silas Reef

Burnout/
Mark Abends

Ace Spandex/
Aaron Khouri

Matross Legion

Not pictured: Harrier, because the writer
forgot to mention him to the artist. Whoops.

ABOUT THAT GUY WHOSE BOOK YOU READ ONCE

Liam Gibbs knew he was destined to write at age four, when he authored a breathtaking account of a cow who ate grass. The bovine saga failed to catch the public's eye but earned the budding author parental acclaim. Since those early times, he's gone on to write the novella *Not So Superpowered* and humorous articles for various magazines.

That one time I was deep in thought and— Hey, is that ketchup on the ceiling?

A twenty-year veteran of the brutal world of hand-to-hand comic book fandom, Gibbs cut his teenage teeth on titles such as *Spider-Man*, *X-Men*, *New Warriors*, and other Marvel comics.

Gibbs graduated college with a degree in professional writing, which included classes on fiction writing and story structure. He lives on the balmy shores of Ottawa, Canada, where he relaxes by watching staggeringly awful horror and science fiction movies. A health and fitness nut, he shoots lasers from his eyes, uses the word *exclusive* incorrectly, and once wrestled an exclusive brontosaurus. True story.

For updates and to make sure I'm not eating potato chips for dinner, do yourself a favor and check this series out online. It's the right thing to do.

Get news at inagalaxyfarfarawRy.com
Keep tabs at bit.ly/iagffa_facebook
Follow at bit.ly/iagffa_twitter
Communicate via homing pigeon at chirp-twiddle-twoo or whatever pigeons say.

To see more sassy In a Galaxy Far, Far AwRy action, please review this book at Amazon.com. The more reviews people write, the better this book's ranking does on Amazon, the more exposure this series gets, the more you help an independent author, and the more I love you for everything you do. It's a long chain of cause and effect that ends with rainbows and sunshine for everyone.

And call your mother more often. She worries, you know.

Manufactured by Amazon.com
Columbia, SC
30 March 2017